Wine Club
Wednesdays

Jan Romes

WINE AND SWEAT PANTS SERIES BOOK 4

Wine Club Wednesdays
(*Wine and Sweat Pants series – Book 4*)
Copyright © 2018 Janice Romes
All Rights Reserved

Cover Design and formatting by Tugboat Design

This book is licensed for your personal enjoyment only. This book may not be resold or given away to other people. If you would like to share this book with another person, please purchase an additional copy for each recipient. If you're reading this book and did not purchase it, or if not purchased for your use only then please purchase your own copy. Thank you for respecting the hard work of this author.

This is a work of fiction. Names, characters, places and incidents are either the product of the author's imagination or are used fictitiously, and any resemblance to actual persons, living or dead, events, or locales is entirely coincidental.

To my family, friends, and readers – with your unyielding enthusiasm and support, you make this crazy thing I do for a living seem perfectly normal. From the bottom of my heart, thank you!

Dear Readers:

Thank you for the encouragement to write book #4 in this series. Creating Elaina, Tawny, Steph, and Grace has been a joy I never could've imagined. They've made me laugh, cry, and commiserate as they discovered the power of true friendship. Starting over in their forties terrified them, but they did it together with long talks, mischief, a smidgen of revenge, exploring their talents, and a little wine. In the mix of all that happiness and chaos, has been Stony the adorable Husky and Lula the cat.

In books #1 and #2, the wine club ladies mentally started over. In book #3, they physically began again in Maine. Investing in their future with the purchase of a bed and breakfast, their gifts really started to shine. Life was full and on track. Soon after the arrival to their new home, some romantic interests happened for each one. And with that, I give you book #4.

What will these four incredible women, Stony, and Lula get into next? Read on and find out. I'm always tickled to get feedback. I hope you'll let me know what you think when you're finished.

Love,
Jan

*Members of the No Sweat Pants Allowed – Wine Club
and owners of the Four Sassy Chicks Bed and Breakfast*

Elaina Ashlynn Samuels

Tawny Piala Westerfield

Stephanie Irene Mathews

Grace Vivian Cordray

Wine Club
Wednesdays

Chapter One

~ Punch the sucker until it works! ~

Elaina cocked her head to the side and grinned at the caricature Philip had drawn of Grace. "He's caught your essence."

"My nose is too big."

"Yes it is." Tawny flicked the tip of Grace's nose.

"Not my nose-nose, on the drawing."

Steph weighed in with a giggle.

Philip stood with his arms crossed. "Relax, Grace, it's a cartoon sketch."

She gave him the evil eye. "Let me draw you."

He met her scowl with a hearty laugh. "Sketch away, gorgeous. I should warn you, I only pose in the nude."

Steph directed an authoritative finger at Philip. "Keep your clothes on." She turned to Grace with a grin. "Control your boyfriend."

"Au naturale is the only way to go." Philip lifted the bottom of his shirt like he was going to strip. It earned him a poke in the ribs from Grace.

Steph splayed a hand over her face and peeked through her fingers. "Some things can't be unseen, Philip. I'm just saying."

Tawny handed out champagne flutes. "The New Year will be upon us in two minutes."

Steph instructed Nick to pop the cork on the bubbly at the stroke of midnight.

Visions of Philip without clothes were forgotten and everyone's attention transferred to the television, where an excited crowd in New York cheered ahead of the ball dropping in Times Square.

Happy tears sprang to Elaina's eyes. Eight months ago, she couldn't have imagined being blessed with three best friends, let alone celebrating New Year's Eve with them in Maine – in the Four Sassy Chicks Bed and Breakfast they now owned. Meeting Tawny, Steph, and Grace had been a blessing in so many ways.

Tawny broke into Elaina's reflection with a similar thought. "Can you believe we moved to New England? It doesn't seem real. Pinch me."

Grace obliged the request with a finger nip to Tawny's arm.

"Owww!"

"You said 'pinch me'."

"I meant metaphorically."

Grace dodged a retaliatory pinch by ducking behind Steph.

Even with the playful antics going on around her, Elaina's thoughts deepened. The fast approaching New Year equaled a fresh start; a chance to fix or tweak things.

A mental list of trivial items that needed mended or restored surfaced, along with two complicated matters that had to be dealt with at some point – one personal, one business. She shook off the personal complication to focus on the business one – the lack of guests. According to the register left behind by the Kirbys – the previous owners – the bed and breakfast last year on New Year's Eve had been booked to the hilt, with a waiting list in case of cancellations. This year, zero guests were there to ring in the New Year. Elaina blamed the weather. It had been snowing almost nonstop since Christmas. This morning the weatherman advised another nor'easter would arrive at the beginning of the week. They were already up to their eyeballs in the white stuff; another round would reach the rooftop. She refused to worry. They'd get their footing and guests would come. Realistically, they needed a creative marketing strategy since there were plenty of lodging choices for folks to pick from. She snapped out of the reverie when Bart, Tawny's beau hunk, started the countdown at the half-minute mark.

When five seconds remained, eight voices joined in the anticipation. "Five, four, three, two, one!" The ball in Times Square fell and they shouted, "Happy New Year!"

Stony added to the celebration with an excited yowl.

A round of hugs commenced.

Nicholas popped the cork on the champagne and had the honor of filling their glasses with the effervescent wine.

Elaina raised her glass and swept her gaze across each person in the room. "The past several months have been a mixed bag of amazement. For four of us, our journey began in a jewelry store in Ohio and we ended up in a bed and breakfast in Maine. We've gone through phenomenal chaos and fun, change and growth."

Chad Ferguson put a hand on the small of Elaina's back. "The men here have had our shares of ups and downs as well. The year got unbelievably better in November, thanks in part to meeting you ladies. Right, guys?"

Nicholas Augustine, Bartholomew Simpson, and Philip Treatwood concurred with a bob of their heads.

"I know the next twelve months will be incredible." Chad placed his lips at Elaina's temple. Stony wedged between them. "Back off, she's mine," he said to the Siberian Husky, and tried to move the dog away with his thigh.

Stony didn't budge.

"I think the dog's jealous."

Tawny refuted Chad's claim. "No he isn't. He's protecting our fearless leader."

"From what? I'm a cop."

Elaina picked up on the tinge of annoyance in Chad's tone and she defended Stonewall Jackson Westerfield. "He's as human as a dog can get and he needs constant personal contact."

Chad raised his eyebrows.

Stony actually belonged to Tawny, yet they all claimed him as theirs. Tawny left Bart's side and came to the sweet pooch. She knelt in front of him and ran her fingertips gently over the velvet fur on his nose. "You're the king of our castle, boy. Don't let anyone," she looked up at Chad, "tell you otherwise."

Chad mumbled something impossible to make out, piquing Elaina's curiosity even more. Surely the well-built, muscled officer of the law wasn't threatened by their love for Stone-man.

Steph announced it was time to dig into the great eats she and Nicholas had prepared. "Instead of sticking with one type of cuisine, like Chinese food or Italian, we made a variety of dishes to please everyone's taste buds."

The restaurant owner in Nicholas took over. "For your dining enjoyment, we've prepared clam chowder, lobster rolls, hot and sour soup, cheese ball, ham and dill pickle rollups, corn casserole, steak bites wrapped with bacon, and a vegetable tray."

Grace inhaled the mouthwatering aromas and her eyes rolled back in her head. "Bring on the goodies."

Bart lifted the lid on one of the Crock pots and made a face. "Does this hot and sour soup have tofu?"

Steph slapped him on the back. "Yeah, buddy, it does. It also has mushrooms."

Grace reminded Steph she had an aversion to both mushrooms and tofu. "Remember our jaunt to that Chinese restaurant in Ohio, where you called me Fungi Wuss?"

Steph's laugh came out as a snort. "Your memory is a tad fuzzy. YOU called yourself Fungi Wuss." She leaned into Grace's personal space and whispered, "It was the same night we brought identical purses and I grabbed yours by mistake, only to discover you had a fun pack of protection in it."

Grace teasingly narrowed her eyes into thin slits. "It was a Trojan Pleasure Pack. I still have the box."

"Well, Fungi Wuss, maybe your New Year's resolution should be to put more pleasure in your life."

Tawny asked why they were whispering.

Neither Grace nor Steph had perfected the art of speaking softly, and Elaina had been close enough to catch every word. She pretended to be interested in the ham and pickle rollups, while she waited to hear if Steph would mention the prophylactics to Tawny.

"Grace is in a panic about the soup. I told her we made a separate pot for those who turn up their noses at things that are good for them."

Grace's light blue eyes gleamed with conspiracy. "I inquired how fungus could possibly be good for me."

Elaina chuckled without making a sound. Any further discussion of condoms was cleverly tucked away.

Ever the nurse, Tawny shared how mushrooms were a good source of copper, potassium, and protein. "Don't get me started on the benefits of tofu. It has protein, all eight essential amino acids, iron, and cal..."

"Thank you, talking-health-journal. I still think tofu tastes like cardboard. And mushrooms?" Grace shuddered. "I can't even. Who said, 'Let's grow these spores in horse manure, watch them grow, and then eat them?'"

"You're such a drama queen, Cordray."

"No I'm not. I'm the quiet one." Grace bared her pearly whites in a mischievous grin. "Bart and I are just picky about what we put in our mouths."

Bart patted Grace on the head. "You know it."

Philip wrapped his arms around Grace from behind and nuzzled her neck.

Elaina studied Philip's move and entertained the notion he didn't want Grace becoming too friendly with Bart. *Hmm.* Not even five minutes into the New Year and two suspicions had surfaced. A deceptive smile curved the corners of her mouth, while internally brakes squealed, airbags went off, and glass shattered at the possibility that she and Grace were involved with men inclined to be possessive.

Tawny surveyed the rest of the food choices and homed in on the cheese ball. "Are those chocolate chips?"

Nicholas beamed a smile of pride. "They are. It's a dessert cheese ball."

"You and Steph are wizards in the kitchen, but meanies when it comes to my waistline."

Steph assured Tawny her waistline was fine. "Mine, on the other hand, has expanded. I love to cook and it shows." She smeared a glob of cheese ball onto a graham cracker. "My New Year's resolution is to get back to an exercise routine. With the move and all, I've become a slacker. Elaina, you helped me once, I need you again. I could use your expertise too, Tawny. This time, I want you both to be relentless. With exercise and healthy food choices," she ran a hand down her side, "this body will be svelte."

Tawny hip-checked Elaina. "Did you hear her? She wants us to be relentless. When we get up in her grill and make her sweat, she'll whine and we'll need wine to cope." She placed a hoagie roll on her plate and topped it with buttery lobster.

"Of course I'll whine. It's to be expected. Since you love me, you'll put up with it and encourage me to keep going." Steph skimmed the full counter. "Today's the last day for this kind of rich food. From now on, it's a lifestyle change to fewer calories and better choices."

Nicholas groaned. "That means one for me too."

"Count on it." Steph stepped on her tiptoes and planted a kiss on his mouth. "I want a body made for sin, but the main objective is good health. I have big plans for us, Nicholas Augustine, and we have to be fit to do all of it. I want us to hike and bike. We'll check out the piers and boardwalks. When the Portland Observatory opens in May, we'll climb the stairs and take in the awesome views of the city and Casco Bay. We'll explore the 47,000 acres in Acadia National Park. Some morning, we'll get up early and watch the sun rise from Cadillac Mountain."

"Reality check, Steph. I'm in my fifties. While I'm in relatively good shape, my knees reject the idea of climbing anything. As far as walking 47,000 acres, yeah, I don't know if it'll happen. I own a restaurant and you're part-owner of a bed and breakfast. We don't have a lot of free time. My wait-staff probably isn't happy with me as it is, for digging out early tonight. When spring, summer, and fall arrives so do the tourists. Business will boom. Aaaand, how can we go forward with our cookbook? We can't create recipes without trying everything we make. I love your body, just the way it is. You have sweet curves."

Steph didn't over-think her reply. "Thanks, Nick," she batted her eyelashes theatrically. "But like it or not, a lifestyle change is going to take place. We'll figure it out. In the meantime, you know what they say about all work and no play."

Nick countered, "You know what they say about women who come up with cockamamie plans."

Everyone laughed, including Steph.

Tawny offered her two cents. "I want in – with the exercise plan and discovering Maine." She failed to mention changing her eating habits.

"Don't leave Grace and I out." Elaina took a celery stick from the veggie tray. "I'll have to pass on anything that has to do with mountains though. I'm still traumatized from hanging off the side of that hill with Stony in my arms." She smiled at Tawny. "If you hadn't found us when you did…"

Chad's eyes doubled in size. "What?"

"Long story short, Stony started to go over a hill and Elaina went after him. They hung there for a good while. As you can see," Tawny gestured to Elaina and then to Stony, "it had a happy ending. I think that's why Stoneman has a special affection for the boss lady."

"He caused you to go over a hill?"

Elaina's temper bubbled up unexpectedly, but she kept it in check. "He didn't cause me to do anything. It was a reflexive action for someone I love."

"He's not someone, he's a dog."

She stood her ground. "He's more than a dog, Officer Ferguson."

Chad put his hands up in surrender. "Okay, okay. I understand."

Elaina doubted he did. She ladled a bowl of hot and sour soup and sat at the table.

Chad heaped his plate with steak bites and joined the other men who'd wandered back to the family room to continue watching the worldwide celebrations.

Tawny scooted a chair close to Elaina's. "Do I detect trouble in paradise?"

"We've never made it to paradise." She slurped a spoonful of soup. "He's a great guy; sexy, intelligent…"

"He has handcuffs."

Normally, Elaina would've chuckled at the insinuation; tonight she wasn't feeling particularly amused. "What's wrong with me, Tawn'? Over the past few days, I've found fault with everything he says or does."

"This is the first I'm hearing about it."

"I haven't said anything until now."

Steph huddled in. "What's going on?"

Grace crunched a carrot stick. Between chews, she offered Steph an answer. "She's clearly not happy with Chad. It's because he hasn't taken to Stony like we have."

Elaina furrowed her eyebrows. "Is that why?"

"You could be having a mid-life crisis." Tawny tapped the side of Elaina's head. "There's a lot going on inside your melon. I've seen it in your eyes."

Steph stole a mushroom from Elaina's bowl. "You could be right, Tawn'. Her birthday's in eleven days."

Grace nodded. "Usually, she's the level-headed one of the bunch. Maybe the midlife crisis witch picks her victims from those who think they're the least vulnerable."

"Helloooo. I can hear you."

"Good. Then we're not talking behind your back." Steph reached for another mushroom.

Elaina flicked Steph's hand away. "This isn't about my birthday."

"If this odd behavior isn't birthday-related, then what's it about?" Grace prodded.

"I honestly haven't pinpointed the cause. It might be Chad. It might not be. I don't know. He's showing a side of him I'm not fond of. When we first met, he acted as though Stony was the bomb. I've discovered that affection was forced. When he thinks I'm not looking, he glares at Stony. And he steers clear of Lula."

"It's the other way around. Lula steers clear of him," Grace clarified. "You have to admit, that cat doesn't play well with most people. She barely tolerates Stony."

Tawny looked around. "I haven't seen her all day."

"She's safely tucked away under the gaudy loveseat you bought."

"Don't diss the purple beast."

A genuine laugh took hold of Elaina. "I wonder who designed that particular piece of furniture."

"Someone very conservative." Tawny offered a cheesy grin. "What can I say? It was an impulsive purchase."

"I tease you about the darn thing, but it's grown on me."

"Good to know." Tawny slanted a wicked grin at Grace. "See how smooth she is? She took the spotlight off her midlife crisis and put it on the loveseat."

"I doubt I'm having a midlife crisis, because I'm not

in midlife. On average, women live to be 86.6 years old."

"Do the math, Einstein. Half of 86.6 is what?" Grace accidentally dropped a graham cracker loaded with cheese ball onto the floor. In a heartbeat, Stony was there to swoop it up with his tongue before she could even make an attempt to pick it up. "Is cream cheese bad for dogs?" Her question hit the air and dissipated when no one paid attention.

"Crap. I've been at the midlife point for a few months."

"Join the club." Tawny chuckled. "I'll be forty-eight in June."

"We're in the presence of geezers, Steph."

Tawny shot an arrow into Grace with her eyes. "You'll turn forty-two next month. The second you snivel and gripe, we'll be all over it. Won't we, Elaina?"

"Oh yeah."

"And Steph, you'll be forty-one in May. So ixnay the wisecracks about our age or you'll suffer the wrath of your elders."

Elaina raised her eyebrows and held them in the up position.

Grace dared the wrath and lobbed another taunt at Tawny, "You mean senior citizens."

"Whatever." The bossy cadence in Tawny's tone said the discussion was now closed. She elbowed Elaina. "Did you hear Arden Wellby Samuels come out of Chad's mouth earlier? Be truthful. It wasn't the first time it's happened."

Elaina winced at the awareness. "You noticed too?"

Steph poked Elaina on the back. "He's not your ex."

Grace picked a chocolate chip out of the cheese ball and popped it in her mouth. "You know he isn't, Elaina. The only thing the two men have in common is they're both hotties."

Tawny sighed. "Why did you bring that up?"

"I stated a fact. Arden and Chad are in fact hot. That's where the similarities stop."

"How did we go from cheering for the New Year to hating mushrooms to midlife crises to Chad sounding like Arden and both being hot?" Elaina groaned and pushed her bowl of soup away. "Does anyone want to go for a walk?"

Steph stretched up to look out the window. "I'm not in the mood to become a snowman."

Grace was quick to point out that no matter how hard it was snowing, Steph didn't have the right equipment to become a snow...man.

Elaina polled the table. "No takers?" Subtle head shakes caused her to mutter, "Wimps." She grabbed Stony's leash and went into the living room. "Chad, would you like to see some snowflakes up close?"

"Uhh..." He appeared more interested in the buxom redhead on TV, who was belting out the lyrics to her latest song. Every time the famous singer moved, her chest heaved up and almost escaped the confines of her sexy, skimpy sequined dress.

Elaina smirked at how laser-focused all the guys were on the singer and how they seemed to be hoping for a wardrobe malfunction. "No worries. I won't be gone long. Come on, Stony-maroni. You and I were made for snow."

"Don't let him drag you off the side of any hills," Tawny quipped.

Lula stuck a paw out from under the purple loveseat and swiped at Stony.

Bart tore his eyes away from the TV long enough to say, "Stony, get the cat." He and Stony had a special bond, thanks to collecting Stone-man when he ran off shortly after they moved to Portland.

Stony eyed Bart for a second and then shoved his nose under the loveseat to get Lula.

Elaina warned Bart with a humorous glare.

He responded with a high-cheek grin. "Not your circus, not your monkeys?"

Elaina glanced at Tawny. "You shared my motto with Bart?"

Mischief sprinted into Tawny's expression. "He had to know about the circus."

* * *

Steph stuck her head in the refrigerator. "What happened to the leftover cheese ball?"

"I tossed it in the trash before we went to bed." Tawny shouldered Steph out of the way to get a cup of dark cherry Greek yogurt.

"Why? Three-fourths of it was left."

"You wanted relentless. You're getting relentless."

"I meant after all the goodies were gone."

"That's not what you said."

Elaina shuffled into the kitchen and blew on her cold hands to try to warm them. Even though she'd worn gloves, her fingers felt like they were one step away from having been frostbitten. Before anyone else had gotten out of bed, she'd taken Stony outside so he could make yellow snow. Then she used the snow blower on the porch, deck, steps, and sidewalk. The effort had been in vain. By the time she finished, the wind kicked up and coated every surface with the same snow she'd removed. "Steph, you look like you're about to spit nails."

"She's ticked at me for throwing out the cheese ball."

Elaina pulled her lips in tight to keep from smiling and commenced pouring a cup of coffee. "I'm having veggies. We have a ton of them left."

"You're as subtle as a blister. Instead of telling me to shut my yapper and have carrot sticks, you cleverly mention what you're having." Steph continued to grumble about the cheese ball that had met an early demise. "It's wrong to waste food."

Tawny shoved a bite of yogurt in her mouth and licked the spoon. "New Year. Same growly stance. We'll have our work cut out for us, Elaina."

"Speaking of work," Elaina removed the vegetable tray from the refrigerator and took a handful of orange pepper slices. "I'd like to have a business meeting sometime today."

Steph's lips skewed into gnarled dislike. "Bell peppers for breakfast?"

"Absolutely." Elaina added crisp sugar peas to the stash.

Grace traipsed in, holding her head. "Who can I blame for this headache?"

Steph pointed both index fingers at Tawny. "She's the culprit."

A sly grin settled into Tawny's face. "I wanted a special New Year's memory with my besties. After the guys left..."

"At four o'clock this morning," Grace groaned.

"After they left – at four o'clock this morning – I felt an extraordinary tug in my heart."

"Induced by too much wine," Steph harped.

"Probably. I wanted us to have a mini-celebration of our own."

"After all the champagne and Merlot, you introduced us to Fireball whisky." Steph stole a cucumber slice and sat down with one leg tucked under her.

"New year, new beverage."

"New year, new headache." Grace rubbed her temples.

"Fireball was tasty," Steph smacked her lips, "but we're not the No Sweat Pants Allowed – Whisky Club."

"Yeah, but..."

Elaina escaped the good natured debate by leaving the kitchen with her mug of coffee. In the sunroom, she stretched out in a padded Victorian wicker chaise and tugged a fuzzy throw over her legs. Outside the snow continued to swirl and dance on the heavy wind. Over a sip of coffee hot enough to remove a few thousand taste buds, she silently owned up to what they'd discussed last night – she might actually have some midlife issues. She refused to identify it as a crisis, because it wasn't. If anything, it was a subconscious readjustment. Of course, being cooped up might have something to do with the overwhelming bout of restlessness taking her over too. Lack of clientele had to factor into the mishmash of agitation. Following another careful sip of Arabica blend, Officer Chad Ferguson streaked through her mind; although, if she was honest, he seldom left her thoughts. Some of her strife could be attributed to him. He hadn't said it, but she knew he wanted more than she was willing to give. Elaina crossed her ankles and then uncrossed them. She shifted in the chaise, trying to find the sweet spot. After fifteen minutes of squirming around, she headed to the fitness room.

Ditching her coffee, she took a bottle of water from the mini fridge and downed a big swig. On the treadmill, she started slow and increased the level every couple of minutes until she was running hard. It felt good to really move. Forty-five minutes later, she was spent and wringing wet.

"There you are." Tawny made a face. "You either have a perspiration problem or you pushed yourself until your pores had no choice but to leak." She gestured to the front of Elaina's t-shirt that had a circle of moisture below the neckline.

"Perspiration problem."

"Fibber."

Elaina powered down the treadmill until the conveyor belt barely moved and her heart rate returned to a normal tempo.

"I'm getting strange vibes from you, woman. Did we

do something wrong?"

"You didn't do a thing. Tawn', we're fine. In fact, the four of us are great."

"That's a relief. There's still something amiss. I know we had a group discussion about it last night, but now it's just you and me. Talk to me, ole sweaty one."

Elaina's shoulders rose in a high shrug. "There's really not much to say."

"You don't regret the move to Maine, do you?"

"Not even a little."

"Then what?" Tawny handed Elaina a towel.

Elaina blotted her face to keep sweat from running into her eyes. "For a few days now, I've combed through everything from the time I met you, Grace, and Steph, until now."

"And?"

"I'm going to upset the apple cart."

"Uh oh. How so?"

"I'm pretty sure I'm going to sever my relationship with Chad." It felt good to say it out loud and mean it.

Tawny's eyes grew in size. "We established that he doesn't like Stony and Lula, but is it enough to make you want to cut ties?"

Elaina dropped her chin to her chest. "There are some things that bother me."

"Is it because he occasionally sounds like Arden?"

Elaina gave Tawny a half-smile and shook her head. "While that's a little disturbing, it isn't the reason. This is more about me than him." She pulled at her bottom lip with her teeth. "I find myself in a peculiar state of mind."

Tawny motioned for her to keep talking.

"I don't want to be in a relationship, Tawn'."

"Maybe if you slept with him you'd change your mind. Sex is a great release, you know. It can smooth off all the jagged edges."

The laugh Elaina emitted contained very little mirth. "I agree sex is a physical release unlike any other, yet I don't want to use Chad to smooth my jagged edges." She winced. "Here's the plain and utter truth – I've had a taste of freedom and I'm not ready to relinquish it. The longer Chad and I are together, the more serious he'll become and I don't want that. I've never been one to quit a relationship, so this is extremely difficult."

Tawny rubbed her chin and studied Elaina. "I get it. I totally do."

"I'm glad one of us does." Elaina untied the laces and toed off her shoes. "For now, I want to center my attention on the bed and breakfast. And while I'm at it, I want to discover the reason my mom was drawn to the sea."

"Soooo, we're to toss out the idea it's a midlife crisis?"

An authentic laughed rifled through Elaina. "Call it whatever you like."

Tawny slung an arm around Elaina's shoulders. "I admire you for knowing what you want and don't want."

"Don't sensationalize my madness. There's a whole lot of doubt in what I think I want and need. Basically, it amounts to hitting the reset-button again."

"Still, it takes a lot of courage to fine tune your life." Tawny made a fist. "Do what you need to do. Punch that reset button until you get the desired results."

Chapter Two

~ *Walk the plank!* ~

Elaina carried in a tray containing a plate of assorted cheeses, a stack of small plates and napkins, along with a crystal decanter of cranberry juice and placed it in the center of the table. "The reason I called this meeting is so we can brainstorm a creative marketing plan. As you well know, our guest numbers have dried up. There's also that one-star review we got from a former guest. We need more guests and more reviews to override the bad one. I know it's still the holiday, but there's no time like the present to tap into your imaginations."

"I've been concerned too," Grace admitted. "Our grand opening was a success. Afterward, we had a couple of great weeks and then bam! A one-star review and no guests." She chuffed out a sigh. "Is it us? Are we not being professional?"

"We're fine." Steph poured four classes of juice and passed them around.

Tawny stood. "I'll address the elephant in the room.

Our trouble stems from Stony and Lula. People shy away because of our pets. Philip talked us into doing a website photo that included them. Maybe it wasn't such a hot idea."

"Don't rag on Philip." Grace gave Tawny a firm look.

"I'm not. I'm just saying Stony and Lula might be keeping guests from coming."

Once again, Grace chimed in. "That's absurd. They're not the reason. Neither is the one-star review. Come on, ladies, think hard. What are we not doing that we should be doing?"

Elaina flipped open a stenographer notebook.

Steph raised her hand. "Let's offer a special – book three nights and get the fourth night free."

Elaina jotted down the information. "Excellent. Let's keep going, roundtable style. Say the first thing that comes to mind, even if it's off-the-wall." She pointed to Tawny. "And go."

"We could do another photo shoot with Philip and sex things up a bit."

Elaina emitted a chuckle. "We're running a bed and breakfast, not a brothel."

"You said off-the-wall, I gave you off-the-wall."

"Right." Elaina wrote down *sex things up*. Although, her idea of sexing things up and Tawny's might not pair up.

"Is there a bed and breakfast association we should be joining?" Steph answered her own question. "I'll look into it."

"Instead of backing off from Stony and Lula, we need

to drive home the fact that we're pet friendly. Four out of five households have pets." Grace indulged in a taste of juice and made a face. "Man that's tart."

"Is that true?" Elaina questioned.

"Yes, the juice is tart."

"Not that, the numbers."

"I may have embellished, but you get the gist of what I'm saying. Lots of folks have pets and don't want to board them when they travel. That has to be a huge plus in our favor."

"You're right as rain and twice as wet, Grace," Tawny teased.

This brainstorming session was pumping Elaina up. "In our travels to get here, we looked for pet-friendly places to stay. We were fortunate to find some, but they were few and far between. So yes, we're going to brag about how we accept pets."

"Even llamas?"

Grace cocked an eyebrow. "That's going to the extreme, Steph."

"Exactly. That's why we need to spell out only cats and dogs are permitted. Someone might show up with a llama or goose."

"I agree. There was a situation a while back, where a lady tried to board a plane with an emotional-support peacock." Tawny ran her fingers through the hair on Stony's back. He lay beside her with his head resting on her foot.

Elaina scribbled down the suggestion and wrote in parentheses (no llamas, ostriches, geese, or peacocks).

"We might want to flaunt the fact that our B & B is within walking distance of the waterfront."

Steph produced a bag of shelled pistachios and dumped them on one of the plates. She tossed a nut into her mouth, with a contemplative look on her face as she chewed. "Our site needs to highlight our fitness center."

Tawny was quick to point out it was a fitness room. "Center implies a huge workout facility."

"Elaina said to be creative."

"Hellooo, we still have to abide by the whole truth in advertising bit."

"We're getting off track. What else can we add to draw attention to who we are and what we have to offer?" Elaina clicked her pen a few times.

"Who we are." Tawny tapped her chin. "Who we are," she repeated. "I'm a nurse. You're a fitness guru. Steph's a secretary slash chef. Grace is a bank teller. Big whoop. Those who browse for a place to stay won't give a rat's arse about any of it."

"That's where our imagination comes into play. Instead of stating you're a nurse, we could list that we have a medical professional on staff."

Mischief rolled off Steph. "Or we could really soup it up by saying we have our own Florence Nightingale with torpedo boobs to assist with your medical needs."

Tawny made the sound of a buzzer going off and then lifted her breasts. "We'll leave these out of our dossier. They might attract the wrong kind of customers." She repeated Elaina's comment. "We're not a brothel, you know."

Steph propped her elbows on the table. "Okay, forget your boobs. I know what Elaina means. We ARE the bed and breakfast. We need to sell the fact we would know what to do in case of a medical emergency, that our fitness instructor can make them sweat if they're into exercise, and my food will excite their taste buds." She shrugged at Grace. "I've got nothing for bank teller."

Grace's lip jutted out in a fake pout. "I'm good with money; therefore, I can suggest to our customers ways to get the best tourist experience without breaking their bank."

"Ohhhh, I like it." Elaina was all smiles.

Tawny grinned big. "Our business is Four Sassy Chicks Bed and Breakfast. In bold print, we could advertise that we are lively, bold, and energetic."

"And that we provide transportation to and from the airport." Grace snickered. "We should also publicize that Steph won't be behind the wheel."

Elaina started to laugh, but stopped. Steph was a horrible driver. When they were in Ohio, she'd given them all white-knuckle moments. "We all have our flaws, even you, Grace. Let's keep our shortcomings out of it and lure people with our attributes."

Grace offered a weak apology to Steph. "Sorry. Your driving skills, or lack thereof, shall remain a secret."

"Yeah, well, you'd better watch the wisecracks or you'll find stool softener in your pudding."

Grace put her palms up. "Forgive me. You're the world's best driver."

Tawny fell off her chair laughing.

Elaina closed the notebook, but opened it back up. "We should tender the idea that we offer entertainment on specified days of the week."

"Stand-up comedy?" Steph glared at Grace with a lopsided smile.

"I thought more along the line of craft making or card playing. We could do Euchre or Cribbage tournaments."

Grace smirked. "What the hell is Cribbage?"

* * *

"Get a load of this sticky note." Steph removed it from the front of the refrigerator and read it out loud. "Be good to you today – let part of that goodness be challenging. Drink more water. Eat less carbs. Do some planks." She took a glass from the cupboard and filled it with water. "Planks. Bwahaha."

"I know, right?" Tawny adjusted her yoga pants and over-large t-shirt. "The *girls* dust the floor when I plank."

Steph laughed at Tawny's pet name for her chest and water spurted out her nose and mouth. "That's a visual you won't see on any exercise video."

Tawny stuck out her tongue. She opened a jar of peanut butter and scooped a spoonful. "A video with only flat-chested, size-three women pushing up off the floor would be borrring, not to mention unrealistic. Women our age have padding and ta-tas."

"A little extra stuffing isn't a bad thing. I'll never be a size three, but I'm going to break my butt to get to an eight. I want to prove to myself I can do it. It'll be a battle, because I'm a foodie. I loooove food."

Tawny fluffed her hair and pulled her shoulders back. "I'm a ten."

Steph rolled her eyes. "Keep dreaming."

"I didn't mean size ten. I meant on the hotness scale."

"I know what you meant. Again, keep dreaming."

Elaina had stepped into the living room at the beginning of Steph and Tawny's discussion and overheard their amusing wordplay. She didn't want to interrupt, but if she didn't get a serious jolt of caffeine soon she wouldn't be responsible for her actions. "Good morning."

"Gahhhh!" Tawny splayed both hands in front of her face, like people who watch horror flicks do.

"What? You've never seen a charcoal mud mask?"

"You look like a ghoul."

"I'm a ghoul in need of coffee." Pouring a cup of dark roast heaven, Elaina blew the steam away and sampled a sip. She smacked her lips and took a seat at the table.

Tawny pointed out that Elaina had accidentally dropped a blob of charcoal mask on her neck.

"It wasn't an accident. I have dry spots I'm trying to exfoliate." She looked around. "This place is in dire need of humidity. When I brush my hair, it crackles. I went through the packet the realtor gave us and found the data sheet for the furnace. It says it's supposed to have a built-in humidifier. Obviously, it isn't enough for a place with three floors."

Steph snapped her fingers. "Your ghouly face just gave me an idea. We could offer facials and moisturizer regimens as part of the guest package – for both women and men. And seaweed wraps. Foot soaks and manicures too."

"My ghouly face," Elaina snickered.

Grace plodded into the kitchen like it took a lot of effort to move her feet. She parted her eye with her fingers. "I'm going to need a nap later."

"Philip zapping your energy?"

"Nah. Cody called at three o'clock; nine o'clock his time."

"Italy is six hours ahead." Tawny stashed the peanut butter jar back in the pantry and took a Granny Smith apple from the bowl on the counter. "You should clue him in that it was the middle of the night."

"He should know, he's from Ohio." Grace yawned. "How soon they forget."

"When will he, Isabella, and Karina move to the states?"

"They have some legal wrangling to get through for Isabella and Karina, since they're Italian citizens. My best guess is they'll have it sorted out by spring." Grace's face turned beet red. She removed her robe, grabbed the electric bill from the counter, and fanned herself with it. "I must be getting sick. I keep getting bursts of heat."

Elaina and Steph shared a knowing look. A while back, Grace had a freak-out session concerning menopause, possibly because she'd been exhibiting some symptoms and didn't want to accept she might be advancing toward perimenopause. Her periods were screwed up half the time and now she was having heat bursts. At forty-one, Grace shouldn't have to deal with that nonsense. Unfortunately, some women got warning signs earlier than others. Elaina felt Grace's forehead. "You don't have a fever."

Grace continued to fan herself. "We can't afford to get sick. Coughing and blowing our noses with guests in residence wouldn't be a good thing."

"We have no guests in residence," Steph clarified. "But we're going to offer pamper packages to draw them."

Grace ran her fingertips over Elaina's mud-plastered cheek. "Are you doing a practice run?"

"She has some dry patches she's exfoliating. I don't get the mud mask bit. When you smear gunk on your face, doesn't it clog your pores?" Tawny wrinkled her nose.

Elaina shrugged. "It's supposed to remove toxins and give your skin a healthy glow."

Tawny snatched her phone from the charging station and snapped Elaina's picture. "That's going on our website."

"No it isn't."

"We're expanding our services, huh?" Grace said, as though letting the information sink in.

"Elaina hasn't given her seal of approval." Tawny shoved the apple slicer down on her Granny Smith and passed out apple wedges.

"You don't need my seal of approval. I'm not the boss, even though I have boss-like tendencies. It's a residual effect from owning the fitness center in Ohio. But I'm not the sole owner of the bed and breakfast. We all have an equal voice. If the majority feels a pamper package is a good idea, we'll give it a go." She borrowed Grace's thought. "We'll have to practice, especially with the seaweed wrap."

Grace asked where they'd get seaweed.

"It's not the slimy seaweed you're picturing," Steph explained. "We can buy body wraps online."

"Are they expensive?"

Elaina was glad Grace mentioned money, instead of her. Great ideas sometimes came with hefty price tags. They had to control the finances coming in and going out, and they had to recognize the profit margin of each effort now that four people would be making their living from the business.

Steph didn't seem to take issue with the question. "I'll find out. If it costs too much, we'll nix the body wrap and focus just on facials, foot soaks, and mani-pedis."

They fist-bumped.

Tawny had an apple slice almost to her mouth, but laid it aside on a napkin. "I propose before we get jiggy pampering others, we pamper ourselves."

"I'm all for getting a pedicure. I don't give my feet enough attention." Steph untied her sneaker.

"Ut, ut. Do not show those ogre toes while we're eating breakfast." Tawny smiled at Steph's raised eyebrow. "We can do mani-pedis after we finish a different kind of pampering that includes getting a flu shot, mammogram, pap test, dental checkup, bone density scan, and dermatology appointment; you know, all the *fun* stuff."

Grace helped herself to another apple slice. "Dermatology appointment?"

"Elaina shouldn't assume those spots are just dry skin."

Elaina frowned and touched her nose. "What are you saying?"

Tawny feigned impish innocence. "I'm ready to plank. Anyone else ready to plank?"

* * *

"I believe you're what people refer to as a masochist, Westerfield." Steph grumbled her way into the Four Sassy Chicks Bed and Breakfast van.

"Wrong. A masochist derives pleasure from inflicting pain onto one's self. I'm more of a sadist, someone who delights in the pain of others." Tawny looked in the rearview mirror. "Doing okay, Samuels?"

"Let me put liquid nitrogen on your nose and neck, and I'll ask you the same question."

"No hating on me. Those pre-cancer cells are history."

"Yeah, yeah." Elaina wanted to frown, but Tawny was right. It had been a good thing to pay the dermatologist a visit. "You're definitely a sadist. My skin looks like someone put out their cigarette on me, the dental hygienist must need bifocals because she kept scraping my gums instead of my teeth, my boobs haven't sprung back to their original shape after getting squished in that boob-vise, and my arm is not happy to have gotten a flu shot."

Tawny swiveled around with a huge, goofy grin. "You didn't complain about the pap test. You must've enjoyed that."

A round of laughter rocked the car.

"We needed those procedures, just not all in one day." Elaina quit harping. "We owe you big, Tawn'. It's easy to put off self-care." Everyone, except for Grace, had griped about having things done to them. "Right, Cordray?"

"What?"

"I said it's easy to put off self-care."

"Yes it is." Grace turned away and looked out the window.

Elaina took a gander at what might be bothering Grace. "When you got your pap test, you asked about perimenopause, didn't you?"

"I wanted to. The words wouldn't come out of my mouth."

"It's a sensitive subject for you, but you have three concerned best friends. While you were tucked away in the exam room, we discussed your dilemma. Tawn' said a salivary test can be done to check your hormone levels."

Tawny chipped into the conversation, "You're not necessarily in perimenopause, Grace. For appearances sake, you are. But stress can mess you up too."

Grace fought the idea with a tight frown. "I'm not under any more stress than the rest of you."

"Wanna bet? Don't bite my head off or start crying when I list a few things. And dammit, look at me when I talk to you."

Grace obeyed the request.

"You're in a relationship with Philip. You really like him, yet you're struggling with the fact you'll always be in love with Brince."

Grace made a soft, whimpering noise.

Tawny continued. "You hate change, but you took a chance and left a secure job and paycheck. You put most of your things in storage and rented out your home to your niece. We moved to Maine. Your son decided to settle down and marry a lovely girl, who happened to have a child. Grace, you became a mother-in-law and grandma the second Cody said his wedding vows. I'd say the combination of everything has your hormones out of whack, most especially your cortisol."

A series of contortions moved across Grace's expression. "I'm not weak. I can deal with the pressure."

Elaina was set to side with Grace that she wasn't weak. She also intended to add that sometimes our subconscious holds onto things longer than it should and sabotages the way our bodies respond. She didn't get a chance to say a word, because Steph charged in with her take on things.

"I don't know about you, but I've had enough *pampering* for one day. We can sit here and bitch about Tawny making us get poked, squeezed, having skin cells freeze-dried, and more. Or we can head to that winery on Thompson's Point and *deal* with a glass of wine. Or we could go home and *deal* with a plank challenge."

Grace bobbed her head up and down. "I'm all for drinking a glass of wine, while I watch Tawny *walk the plank*."

Chapter Three

- Hot Stuff! -

Elaina headed back to the table from the ladies room and smiled when their waitress fell into step with her.

"You own the Four Sassy Chicks Bed and Breakfast."

"We do."

"Well, I'm happy to say you're the talk of the town." The sixty-something waitress balanced a charcuterie tray on her hip and leaned to look past Elaina.

Following the woman's line of vision, Elaina's eyes landed on their van parked outside a large picture window. "I hope the gossip is good."

"Rave reviews, absolutely. The name you picked implies snarky entertainment."

"There's no denying we're a bit peculiar, but we're just four women whose personalities blend well." Elaina's gaze swept to her three friends. Some might view what they said and did as entertainment; truthfully they were just being themselves.

"I also heard you have a top-notch chef on staff."

"You've been talking to Nicholas."

"It's hard not to talk to Nick. He's a type-A personality and passionate about business. I assume you're here at his recommendation."

"Actually, our chef suggested the visit."

"So you do have a chef?"

To say Steph was gifted in the culinary arts was an understatement, although she didn't have the certification or degree to be considered a chef. "We have a kitchen goddess, yes." She wanted to humble-brag that Steph and Nick were co-authoring a cookbook. It wasn't her place or the right time to put the word out.

Just before they reached their table, the waitress clutched Elaina's arm to impede their progress. "I wanted to ask you about the private residence you have in back of the bed and breakfast. Do you rent it out for extended stays?"

Elaina was surprised by the question. "Do you mean by the week or month?"

"I have a nephew who would like a place to lay low for a while."

Instantly, a vision of someone trying to duck law enforcement or hide because they'd ticked off the wrong person came to mind. "Because?"

"Wording is everything, isn't it?" The waitress emitted a small laugh. "I shouldn't have said he wants to lay low. He's a divorced musician who's lost his edge. He's in search of a quiet space to recover his creativity and finish the album he's been working on for a year."

They needed customers in a big way. If this guy could

regain his footing by staying in the loft apartment out back, it would be great for business. After he achieved success with his album, he might spread the word about their place. "I'll give you my business card. Have him call and we'll work something out."

"Excellent." The wooden board filled with goodies was placed in the center of the table. "Ladies, your charcuterie." The waitress pointed to the cheeses. "Goat Gouda, Brillat Savarin, Parmigiana-Reggiano, and Gorgonzola Dolce."

Tawny's eyebrows shot up. "Say what?"

"Goat Gouda is a mild goat cheese. Brillat Savarin is creamy brie. Parmigiana-Reggiano has a more complex flavor. I can only describe it as nutty and sweet. Taste it and see what you think. The Gorgonzola Dolce is sweet, creamy, and easy to spread."

"No, I meant what is charcut..." Tawny snagged a black olive from the board. "What's the word again?"

Steph butted in with an answer. "Charcuterie. It's French."

"For meat and cheese tray?"

"Actually, charcuterie refers to any smoked, dry-cured or cooked meat," Steph clarified as though she had a dictionary at her fingertips.

The waitress agreed with a nod. "You have to be the chef."

Steph queried Elaina with her eyes.

"Your reputation is bouncing around Portland, Steph."

Steph nervously wrung her hands. "I'm more of a hack than a chef."

"Would you listen to her downplay her talent? I used to despise succotash. The way Steph makes it, I fill my plate."

"Elaina's not lying. She wolf's it down like it's caviar." Tawny's subsequent grin was filled with mischief.

"I don't *wolf* anything down. Geez, Tawn'."

"Forgive me." Tawny rolled her eyes. "You daintily enjoy succotash."

The waitress laughed so hard she had to put her hands on her stomach to stop it from jiggling. "Four Sassy Chicks fits you ladies to a tee."

Grace placed a napkin across her lap and took a pickle from the selection of delights.

"The pickles are tangy and the pate is to die for. The black olives are just as they should be, but I have a warning regarding the green olives – they're packing some heat. They're stuffed with jalapenos."

A bus boy delivered a basket of thinly sliced French bread.

"Okay, ladies, you have your wine and charcuterie plate. I'll be back in a few minutes to check on you. In the meantime, enjoy."

Elaina handed her their business card. "Could I ask your nephew's name?"

"Rob Blakefield."

"Rob Blakefield. Rob Blakefield," Grace repeated. "Where have I heard that name?"

Elaina smiled up at the waitress. "We look forward to hearing from him."

The second they were alone the grilling began.

"We look forward to hearing from him?" Grace reached in front of Elaina to snatch a piece of bread.

"Our waitress has a nephew who might be interested in renting the loft. He's a musician."

Steph popped a green olive-jalapeno into her mouth. "Yowza! She wasn't kidding. You get a burst of flavor and heat."

"Hand me one." Tawny eased it into her mouth. "Holy mackerel! I may have to apply burn cream to my tongue." She tried to douse the blaze with wine. "That didn't help a bit."

"And the drama queen crown goes to Tawny." Grace swiveled her focus back to her inquiry about the musician. "Is Rob Blakefield as hot as those olives?"

"I have no idea."

"What kind of music does he play?"

"What you know about Rob Blakefield is what I know." Elaina took a slice of bread and topped it with Brillat Savarin.

"I know I've heard his name before." Grace licked her lips after sampling the Gorgonzola Dolce. "Delish'." She took another bite. "We have to buy some of this. In the meantime, Tawny Pia, use your phone and track down Rob Blakefield."

"It's Tawny Piala."

"Excuse em wa. Tawny Piala, please Google Rob Blakefield."

"That's better, Grace Vivian." Tawny messed with her phone and kept refining the search. "There are some Robert Blakefield's, Roberto Blakefield's, Ron

Blakefield's, a Russell Blakefield, but no Rob's."

"Did you type Rob Blakefield-musician?" Steph asked innocently, which garnered a glare from Tawny.

"It's not my first Google search."

Grace braved repercussions and stole Tawny's phone. "Let me."

Tawny winced. "You're lucky we're friends."

Grace pecked away and came up empty too. "I think our waitress might be trying to pull a fast one. I cannot find a Rob Blakefield who makes music."

"She didn't say he was famous."

"What *did* she say?" Grace handed the phone back.

"That he was a divorced musician."

"Divorced from his wife or from his music?" Steph plucked a black olive from the stash.

"She meant divorced-divorced. He wants a quiet place to lodge. We'll give him one."

Tawny made a face when she tasted the Parmigiana-Reggiano cheese. "Blech."

"Not to your liking, Piala?"

"What's with you today? Did someone dial your heckle-ometer to the highest setting?"

Elaina poured more Raspberry Merlot into her glass and passed the bottle. "I don't know about the rest of you, but I'm hoping hard-to-find Rob decides to stay with us."

Steph snorted a laugh.

"What?"

"When you said hard-to-find Rob, my mind pictured the *Where's Waldo* guy."

"You've either had too much wine or those olives have something other than jalapenos in them."

* * *

Dressed in a white, satiny, full-length puffy coat that made her look like the Michelin man, Grace strolled through the living room where Elaina, Tawny, and Steph had their noses buried in books. "I'm headed out."

Elaina looked up from Nora Roberts' latest novel. "It's snowing like crazy."

Grace winked. "I'll be careful, Mother Hen."

Tawny uncurled from the purple loveseat. "Going to Philip's?"

"I am."

"Whatcha got under the coat?" Steph teased.

"I have clothes on, if that's what you're asking."

Steph was all over the situation with a raised eyebrow. "Why do I get the feeling they're very skimpy clothes?"

In a heartbeat, Elaina, Steph, and Tawny set chase. Grace sprinted into the kitchen, ran into the dining area and around the long table, and hurdled over Lula who unintentionally scampered into the good-humored fray. "Don't you hellions have something better to do?" Grace darted to the breezeway in hopes of making a clean getaway.

Tawny grabbed a handful of coat and stopped Grace in her tracks.

Grace's face turned a dark shade of mortified and held the coat snuggly against her front.

"Steph, your hunch may be spot on. Grace is either stark naked or has insufficient coverage." Without releasing her hold on the coat, Tawny made a swipe for the zipper.

Grace batted at Tawny to no avail.

"Leave her alone." Elaina painted on a Mother Henish expression. "You're your own woman, Grace. If you want to prance around without a stitch on, that's your business. But here's something to consider – the roads are icy. Should you have a fender bender and the police get involved, it'll be hard to explain why you won't take your coat off at the police station. If they pat you down at the scene..." She let the thought hang and made her way back to the couch to commence reading.

Grace chopped Tawny's arm to make her let go. "Can't a girl let her hair down without getting the third-degree?" She stomped to the stairs, unzipped the coat, and flashed them. Dressed in a sexy, low-cut pink tankini with no bra and a black-miniskirt, she frowned.

"Is this Philip's idea?" Surprisingly, there was no trace of humor in Tawny's tone.

"He wants to paint me."

"Will the painting be for his enjoyment only? Or are you comfortable showing your areolas to the whole world?"

A panic stricken look flashed across Grace's face. "You can't see them, can you?"

Tawny let silence answer for her.

Grace advanced up the stairs. Over the banister at the second floor, she spilled her guts and there was a noticeable quiver in her voice. "All my life, I've followed the rules; mostly anyway. Suddenly, I have a desire not to. In no way do I want to be slutty, yet I want a taste of the wild side. I want to experience the rush of being naughty – just once."

"Naughty?"

Elaina gave Tawny the leave-it-alone look. "I understand where you're coming from Grace. I'm there too – some days. If Tawny and Steph are truthful, they are as well. It has to be the realization that we're in our forties. Subconsciously, we're fighting it. In my opinion, every woman...and man, for that matter...goes through something similar." She placed a hand across her heart. "My body says I'm in my twenties. My cerebral cortex says 'you wish'. So I really do comprehend where you're coming from."

"But?"

"Proceed with caution."

"You're not telling me to stop being a dunce?"

"I'm not your mother or your conscience."

A tiny smile came forth from Grace. "Thank you. I think I'll change my shirt."

Chapter Four

~ Fermented cabbage, hamsters, and a lion tamer! ~

Tawny sidled next to Elaina with a basket of laundry. "What's with all the clanging and banging in the kitchen? I could hear it from my bedroom."

"Steph's making homemade sauerkraut."

"On purpose?"

"She's committed to her New Year's resolution and eating-well apparently will involve sauerkraut."

"Here we go again. Remember the gassing incident in that elevator? We were headed to the steakhouse in the mall to celebrate the four of us moving in together."

"How could I forget?" Elaina jiggled with a laugh.

"Steph and her binges. She almost exterminated us with noxious fumes after trying to eat her weight in broccoli. I don't even want to think how it'll be with sauerkraut." Tawny plugged her nose.

"Yeah, good times."

The landline phone rang in the kitchen. Tawny

dropped the laundry basket and made a beeline to answer it. "Four Sassy Chicks Bed and Breakfast, Tawny speaking. Yes she is. One moment please." She covered the mouthpiece. "It's for you, Elaina Samuels."

Elaina mouthed the word, "Salesman?"

Tawny shook her head. "Loft dweller."

Awesome. This could possibly be the spark they needed to get their year up and running. "This is Elaina. How can I help you?"

"Jess Blakefield here. I understand you may have a place I can rent."

"Jess Blakefield? Do you happen to also be Rob Blakefield?"

A masculine chuckle traveled through the phone line. "Old habits linger. Aunt Carol still calls me Rob. My dad and I happen to share the same name, with the exception of Junior at the end of mine. These days it's easier to go by my middle name."

"Ah, Jess Blakefield." Elaina quietly snapped her fingers for Tawny to do a fast Google search.

Within seconds, Tawny found him. She flashed four fingers and then six, to indicate he was forty-six. "He's a musician all right." She shoved the cell phone in front of Elaina's face.

Jess was sitting at a black baby grand piano, with a saxophone and trumpet propped against it. He had a thick head of prematurely grey hair; on his nose sat a pair of reading glasses. Elaina had conjured up a vision of him beforehand. She'd pictured him resembling a member of the Rolling Stones, or at the very least, David Bowie.

He didn't look anything like them. "We have a private bungalow in back of the bed and breakfast you might be interested in. It's secluded behind a row of pine trees."

"It sounds perfect."

"Would you like to schedule a time to check it out?"

"Is right now okay?"

Elaina's eyes dropped to the tattered Luther Vandross t-shirt she'd had for the past twenty-five years. It was so threadbare that if you held the fabric to the light, you'd be able to see through it. But it was so much more than a worn out piece of clothing. It was a cherished memory. As a high school graduation gift, her parents had flown them to Seattle to visit her Aunt Vernene and the four of them attended one of Luther's concerts. Even though it was a great shirt, greeting a potential guest in it didn't portray her as professional. To top off her frumpy look, she was having a bad hair day. She'd pulled her unruly locks up into a messy-style bun; which was actually more messy than stylish. "Now would be fine."

"Excellent."

Thinking she had five or ten minutes, Elaina scrambled to the stairs, hoping to do a quick change. At the second step, the doorbell rang.

Tawny and Steph smirked from the archway of the kitchen.

"That's the fastest she's moved in months," Steph quipped.

"Tell me about it," Tawny seconded.

"This has nothing to do with him. We're business women. We should look the part."

"Are you buying that drivel, Steph?"

"Nope."

Elaina gave them a slit-eyed look. Another ring of the bell prompted her to shift to the front door. Before opening it, she straightened her shirt and tucked wayward strands of hair back into the bun. "Welcome, Jess." Pointing to the two yahoos still lurking in the archway, she introduced Tawny and Steph.

Grace chose that moment to peer over the banister. She gave the newcomer a princess-like wave. "Howdy."

Jess gave her a smile and skipped his gaze to Tawny and Steph, and then rested it on Elaina. A slow grin crimped the corners of his mouth. "The sassy chicks."

"They are. I'm not." Elaina laughed herself to the coat closet and grabbed a quilted jacket.

Tawny informed her that the sign out front said four sassy chicks, not three.

"The guy who painted it made a mistake. I specifically told him three."

"I can tell already that this will be quite an experience."

Elaina met Jess's eyes. "Your aunt said you wanted quiet."

"When I'm working, absolute quiet is a must."

Grace stated the obvious, "A guy can't work 24/7."

"My aunt also said you make great food and the entertainment value alone is worth the stay."

"Our reputation precedes us," Tawny boasted.

Steph spoke up about the food. "We make amazing breakfasts and provide a snack that could be considered a light lunch. Dinner is on you."

"Is there any way we could strike an arrangement that would include dinner? I can't cook to save my soul. Having take-out delivered is an option, but that gets old."

"It's okay with me." Steph surveyed each woman to get approval. "Tawn', Grace, Elaina?"

Without hesitation, she received approval from Tawny and Grace.

Elaina was always the veritable cog; geared to weigh the pros and cons. Striking a special deal with Jess would set a precedent. Others would catch wind of it and possibly want one tailored for them. Plus, it might tick off the other owners of bed and breakfasts. Her inner-critic dropped a subliminal brick on her foot – *stop trying to sabotage your success*. As though her mouth had a mind of its own, she blurted, "We're flexible."

"Took you long enough." Tawny crossed the room and tapped Elaina on the head. "Did the hamsters get stuck on the wheel?"

"Don't they always?" She grinned impishly at Tawny, but she gave Jess her business smile. "First things first – let's check out the loft. If it isn't what you're looking for, there's no point in making a dinner agreement."

"The sooner I get situated, the better. There's a lot of madness going on in my head." His eyes flared open as though he realized it made him sound like a serial killer. "The hamsters," he paused, "are up to some musical madness."

"I don't want to hinder the hamsters by delaying your creativity." And that included their own creativity to get customers to come. She had to stop being a cog. Elaina advanced to the kitchen and through the breezeway, with Jess fast on her heels. Stepping outside, her foot caught an icy patch on the deck and her feet went out from under her.

Jess wrenched his arms around her to keep her from wiping out. "Careful there."

As cold as it was, embarrassment flamed heat into Elaina's cheeks. "Sorry about that. I shoveled and scattered salt. Somehow I missed a spot."

"No worries. It could happen to anyone."

Elaina was grateful that Jess moved them from the awkward moment by stating their place was incredible.

"Even with all the snow piled up, it's great." He used his phone to take a few pictures.

"We moved here in November, so we're eager to see how it looks in the spring."

"It's quite different from the Buckeye State."

"You're familiar with Ohio?"

"I know it well. I was born and raised in Dayton."

They proceeded up the curved, brick sidewalk leading to the secluded bungalow.

"No kidding? We're from Cherry Ridge."

Jess pulled the collar of his leather jacket up around his neck. "I've been through Cherry Ridge. I have cousins who live near there."

"Small world. How'd you end up in Maine?"

"When my father decided to take a job overseas, my mom and I moved here to temporarily live with my aunt. Thirty years later, we're still in Maine and my father remains in Thailand."

Elaina didn't know what to say. "That had to be difficult for you." She shoved the key in the lock and opened the door.

Jess shrugged with a faraway look in his eyes. "He comes home twice a year and we've been there a number of times. We're a strange family, but there are stranger."

"Definitely." She gestured for him to enter.

He removed his hiking boots and padded around in his socks. Elaina gave him big points for not tracking snow all over the hardwood floors. She toed off her half-boots and joined him in the center of the great-room.

"Ohhh a slab stone fireplace. Is it real?"

"I'm sorry, it isn't. The original owner chose to have electric fireplaces installed; possibly for cleanliness and liability reasons. Our insurance carrier was happy to know they're electric. It's not as cozy as a wood burning fireplace, but I hope it'll give you a sense of tranquility, and in turn, your creativity will go nuts." She straightened a picture of Canadian geese in flight. "I'm not sure where you do your best work. Let's move on to the bed..." Elaina stumbled over her words. "To the other rooms." She dropped her attention to the slats in the floor, wondering why she was nervous. "We use a microfiber mop and special spray on the hardwood floors. Don't worry about floor care. We'll take care of it." She looked up and saw amusement dancing across his expression.

"Relax. I know you didn't mean to suggest my talent shows up in the bedroom." There wasn't an ounce of cocky in his smile.

"Sometimes the stuff that comes out of my mouth is

a surprise, even to me."

Jess stared at her for an overly long moment. "The second I laid eyes on you, I got the feeling we've met before. I'm sure we haven't, but you look familiar."

"I get that a lot." Elaina traipsed to the kitchen and opened the refrigerator. "We've stocked the refrigerator with essentials – catsup, mustard, mayonnaise, and bottled water. In the cabinets you'll find pots and pans, dishes, and the most important thing a can of coffee."

"Coffee and music get me through the day."

"What kind of music do you sing?"

"Unless you count the disasters I belt out in the shower, none." He rushed to clear up her confusion. "I write lyrics and compose music for jazz, rhythm and blues, pop rock, indie rock, and commercial jingles. I noticed your Luther Vandross t-shirt. Are you a big fan of his work?"

"I am." She went on to explain about seeing him in concert and how she owned every album he ever made.

"You have good taste."

"My taste varies according to my mood. Some days I'm all about Luther; others, I can't get enough of Ed Sheeran, Neil Diamond, Taylor Swift, Outkast, Imagine Dragons, Sam Hunt, and everything in between. I wonder if I've listened to anything you've written."

The corners of his mouth turned up until a smile almost touched his ears. His blue eyes beamed with pride when he shared the names of the musical artists he'd written songs for.

"I'm impressed."

"Don't be. It's their voices that give the songs magic."

"Without the words and musical accompaniment, they wouldn't have a song to sing."

Jess propped against the wall at the stairway. "Thank you. You'll soon find out I'm just a guy who loves everything about music, except the limelight."

"And you came here to create something spectacular, without all the hoopla the public is known to give?"

"It's the basis for my wanting to stay here, yes. I also have some personal things to work through. My cousin recommended you."

"I thought you came on your aunt's suggestion."

"I did. Aunt Carol heard about you and she called my cousin in Ohio to verify the gossip was true."

Elaina snorted at the far-fetched explanation, but tried to cover the noise with a cough. She didn't want to cut the flow of information by keying on what gossip he'd heard. She hoped he'd offer it without her asking.

"My main motivation for being here is to soak up the quiet. As I've said, there are other objectives too." He shifted in place. "Last year was a tough one. I got divorced and my daughter went off to college in Virginia. Empty nest syndrome hit me almost as hard as being single again. Alyssa is my pride and joy, and suddenly she wasn't there. I felt like I'd fallen into a black hole and my music suffered. But when she calls, she sounds happy and that's all a father wants for his child." He raised his palms. "So here I am, trying to fight my way out of the black hole."

"You've come to the right place. We're well aware

of the difficulties that come with starting over. Tawny, Steph, and I are divorcees. Steph doesn't like to think of herself as one though. She was married for a month and doesn't think the label applies to her, but she's had relationship difficulties too. Grace is a widow."

"I'm glad you had, and still have, each other to get through the insanity."

"It's definitely insanity to the nth degree when you don't know what to do. Suddenly you're thrust into," she used his words, "a black hole." This wasn't an easy conversation to have with someone newly-met, but these types of discussions were fast becoming the norm. The personal exchanges started when she bumped into Grace, Tawny, and Steph, and ballooned out to include Michael Rexx – the guy she dated for a short time after her divorce, Norma the waitress from that restaurant in eastern Pennsylvania, the older gentleman in the jewelry store that sold her the anchor necklace, and just about everyone she met these days. For years, she had no one to open up to, now it seemed as though people were strategically placed in her path for that very reason.

"I had my mom and aunt and a few close friends. They helped, but they couldn't quite grasp why I was in such a funk. In their eyes, I should've embraced the independence. I wish it would've been that simple. It wasn't and I turned to the wrong kind of comfort to survive."

Please don't say with booze or drugs. Elaina would never judge anyone who turned to those vices to get through the anguish dealt to them, but once hooked, it made coping problematic. Her expression must've conveyed that thought.

"I soothed myself with food. I'm now fifty pounds overweight. My doctor isn't happy with me. To add insult to injury, I'm teetering on the cliff of pre-diabetes. I've been told it can be reversed if I eat better and exercise."

"You came to our bed and breakfast to get back on track."

"No. I came to you for help."

Elaina was mildly stunned. "I don't understand."

"Whatever the cost of renting the loft, I'll pay twice the amount to get fitness advice."

"That would be gouging. We'd never consider such a deal. We'll be happy to help you in any way we can."

"Not them. You."

"Umm, okay. I'd be delighted, but you have to fill in a few blanks. How does your cousin know me? Was she a member at my fitness center?"

Jess left enough empty space in the conversation to answer her question five times. "Rachel's my cousin."

Elaina was floored. "Rachel? As in the Rachel we befriended at the winery? As in Arden's fiancée?"

Jess's eyelids drooped to hood his blue eyes. Out of caution that Elaina might blow a gasket to know he was related to the new woman linked to her ex?

Rachel had called on Thanksgiving to deliver the bombshell that she and Arden were engaged. At the same time, she shared news that his father was in the hospital fighting for his life due to a blood disorder. Elaina had texted back and forth with Arden for several days after

Thanksgiving to get updates on his dad, but he'd gotten pissy with her after one of the texts. It stopped the flow of communication and she hadn't heard from him or Rachel since. They couldn't be too ticked if they sent Jess her way. The whole Arden-Rachel-Jess scenario seemed unnatural, but hey, anything involving her former husband was a little twisted. "Rachel's a sweet gal."

"That happens to be married to your ex husband."

Elaina instinctively wrinkled her nose. "They actually went through with it? Good for them."

"Sore spot?"

"Not even."

"Are you sure?"

"Absolutely. It's just that I can't picture the two of them together. Rachel's so nice and he's so... Well, enough about that. There's no point in dragging Arden through the mud." *At least without him being hooked up to the back of a plow.* "Rachel recommended me to personally help you?"

"She said you would be firm when it came to an exercise schedule and you'd pressure me to eat better."

"You're straddling the pre-diabetic line, I can't be gentle." Elaina had to put it out there that she could be tough. "For the record, Tawny's a nurse. She has more knowledge on the subject and should coach you instead of me."

"Rachel told me you'd say that. I agree Tawny would be medically in tune with my condition." His tone took on an almost sensuous tone. "But I want you."

A warm shiver coursed through Elaina. To deal with

the sensation, she took a commanding stance. "Then you shall have me...to crack the whip." She couldn't believe she was being so brazen with her choice of words.

They both laughed.

"Up the stairs, mister." Elaina gestured to the bedroom.

"Already getting tough with me." He gave her a playful salute. "Drill sergeant."

"Steph gave me that same title in Ohio when she first wanted to get into shape."

He beamed a serious look. "We all need that one person, Elaina."

Elaina cleared her throat at this stranger's faith in her and because there were some weird feelings going on within her that she couldn't quite identify. "You're going to love the loft. It's comfy up there and French doors open to a balcony."

Tawny came in with all the grace of a herd of buffalo, stomping her snow covered shoes at least ten times on the rug. "Your cell phone has been going berserk." She tossed it to Elaina. "A word of warning – the psycho that keeps calling is the barracuda."

"We were just talking about him."

Tawny's satin brown brows bumped together as if to ask, "You told Jess about Arden? Already?"

Elaina responded to Tawny's unspoken inquiry, "Rachel is Jess's cousin."

"No kidding?"

Jess snickered.

The phone rang again.

Elaina gave Jess a half-smile. "This might take a while.

Tawn', would you finish the tour?"

"I'd be happy to. Come on, Pavarotti."

"I don't compose operas."

Tawny winked at Elaina and looped her arm through Jess's. She proceeded to enlighten him that she was in awe of him after reading his online bio. "You're a genius, just like Pavarotti."

Elaina chuckled. Thank goodness for Tawny's over-the-top personality – it kept her from wanting to bite into the ferocious fish she now had to converse with. "Hello, Arden. Long time no talkie-talkie." He hated slang – that's why she used it with him. She pictured him frowning. "I understand you've been burning up the phone line to talk to me." She winced when she remembered his father was ill. If Arden was calling to inform her that his father had passed, then toying with him was inappropriate. About to backtrack and apologize, Arden's loud exclamation jarred her silent.

"You have to take this dog!"

* * *

"You're leaving something out."

Elaina moved her head back and forth, still flabbergasted at the phone call. "I'm not."

Grace's light blue eyes darkened. "He didn't say, 'Hi, how are you?' or 'Elaina, I need a favor?'"

"Nope. His usual bossiness seeped out of the phone to slime things up."

"What did you say?"

"I told him to put Rachel on the phone."

"Did he?"

"That would entail him actually listening, which he did not. He said, and I quote, 'I helped you, now you have to help me. Come and get this mongrel. He's chewed two pair of my Salvatore Ferragamos.'"

Grace fist-pumped. "Yes!" She took the delight down a notch. "To clarify, Ferragamo makes a great shoe. I'm just tickled that Arden has to purchase new ones; a little comeuppance for being a jerk."

"He told Rachel he was going to get the dog's teeth pulled. When she squawked, he said the only other option was to drop her off at the shelter. She suggested he call me."

"Someone needs to put knockout drops in Arden's coffee and remove HIS teeth." Grace's dark brows formed a strict V. "What constitutes him helping you?"

Elaina sighed. "He's taking credit for sending Jess here."

"He would." Grace pulled the cork on a bottle of Merlot and poured them a glass. "So what's the plan? It's not like you live five minutes away and can rush over to rescue the poor pooch from his dog-hating clutches."

"I'm going to fly to Ohio, give Arden a swift kick in the gluteus maximus, hug Rachel and whisper how sorry I am that she got reeled into his world. Then I'm going to bring the adorable Pomsky home."

Grace stretched her mouth with a noiseless wince.

"I know we already have a dog that drops hair with every step he takes and an independent cat who thinks she owns the place, but I won't allow Arden to use the dog to make Rachel miserable."

"We tried to warn her."

"We did, but the part of the brain responsible for love..."

"Is the temporal lobe." Tawny hung her coat on a hook in the breezeway. "We seem to discuss parts of the brain a lot."

Grace instructed Tawny not to revisit the ridiculous brain conversation they'd had during the drive from Ohio to Maine.

"You're the one who brought it up." Tawny put up her palms. "Why would I want to make you remember that you refused to drink water on the trip, because you didn't want to make additional pee stops? As a result you got dehydrated and I happened to mention when you don't drink enough water, the fluid sack cradling your brain gets depleted."

Grace rubbed her forehead. "Anyhoo, we've just had a few sips of wine and came to the conclusion that the temporal lobe sometimes jades clear thinking."

As always, Tawny offered a unique spin. "Penises do the same thing."

Elaina burst out laughing and Merlot misted the table by way of her nose.

Grace went in to a Ha, ha frenzy. It was as if her internal hard drive malfunctioned and she couldn't get beyond that word. Finally, whatever was stuck cleared. When she looked at Tawny, she went into another robust round of laughter.

"Penises really aren't that funny, unless they're shaped

weird, like an umbrella. Then they're freaking hilarious."

"Tawn', stop." Elaina grabbed a dish cloth and ran it across the table.

"Why are you talking about temporal lobes anyway?"

"One word: Arden." Grace took an unfeminine slurp of wine.

"Arden and temporal lobes. I don't get it." Tawny took a goblet from the hanging rack under the cabinet and filled it to the very top with wine. "Want to bring me up to date?"

Elaina ran her finger around the rim of her glass. "The barracuda ordered me to take his dog."

Tawny cocked her head to the side. "He did what?"

"You heard right. The phone call was to bully me into taking his dog."

"And she's going to do it," Grace added.

Tawny fought the idea. "No she isn't."

"Oh, but I am."

"Why?"

Grace jumped in with both feet. "She says for Rachel's sake."

"Lame."

"Tawnnnn'," Elaina warned.

"I know the real reason. I could be wrong, but I don't think I am. You're going to rescue the pup so you can find out what's going on with your ex. Am I right? Or am I right?" Tawny said cockily, and then pointed to Elaina. "Ready. Go."

"Ready, go, what?"

"I'm giving you an opening to deny the truth."

Elaina slowly blinked. "I can always count on you to get to the heart of the matter."

Tawny shrugged. "I'm just saying if Arden had been mine, which I thank my lucky stars he wasn't, I'd want a glimpse of his new life. It's perfectly normal to want to see how things are going. Part of you wants him to crash and burn, the other part cares about Rachel."

"Maybe."

"When do you intend to go?"

"In a few days, maybe a week."

"Ert!" Grace swatted Elaina on the arm. "Dropping everything for Arden is a gigantic mistake."

"You're right, it is. Regardless, I'm headed to Ohio."

"I'd go with you, but I'm scheduled to do PRN work at the hospital all week," Tawny grumped.

Steph opened and closed the gate they had installed to keep the animals out of the kitchen.

Stony showed his disappointment by dropping to the floor with a thud.

"I caught the tail end of the conversation. Who's going where?"

Grace yanked her thumb toward Elaina. "She got suckered into taking Rachel's Pomsky."

Steph frowned straight away. "Instead of four bitches around here, there will be five?"

It was Tawny's turn to laugh and snort. "Let's recap: we'll have a cat, one male dog, hamsters, and five bitches. Now all we need is a clown and lion tamer to complete our circus."

Steph was confused. "What's that about hamsters?"

Chapter Five

~ *Funky bean dip!* ~

The thing about a room lined with mirrored-walls, you could see every movement, every facial expression, and every attempt to slack.

"Pick up the pace, Mathews."

Steph had been on the treadmill for half an hour and the first droplet of sweat had yet to dot her forehead.

"I'm easing into the physical part of my svelte body plan."

"Your speed level is still at two. Bump it up to three and see what happens."

"Bump it up to three and see what happens," Steph mocked.

Elaina checked Jess's reaction in the mirror. It looked as though he desperately wanted to laugh. His lips were pressed so tightly together, they almost disappeared. Unlike Steph, he was doing remarkably well on his treadmill. He'd hit his stride at level four and the strong muscles in his legs revealed he wasn't as out of shape as he thought. His problem areas were centered at his waist and chest. He'd tried to soothe the hurt of a failed marriage with the wrong kinds of food, and in turn, his insulin numbers sent out an S.O.S. Now he had his work cut out for him. "Doing okay, Jess?"

"I think so."

He wasn't struggling to breathe when he spoke and his face wasn't overly red from the strain. "Check your heart rate."

Jess put his thumb on the heart-shaped button on the treadmill keypad and read the number. "Is that good?"

Elaina scanned the chart attached to the mirror in front of the treadmills. "Let's see, you're forty-six. Excellent. Your heart rate is at eighty-percent."

"Should I keep going?"

"It's only your second day. Each time you work out, we'll add more time. Power down to level three and walk for a few minutes. Repeat the pattern for levels two and one. When you step off the treadmill, your resting heart rate should be back to normal and your legs shouldn't feel rubbery. Tomorrow you can add a fifteen minute stint with weights, if you want to." She swiveled her attention to Steph. "You're barely moving on that thing. What's the deal?"

"The deal is that I don't want to exert all my energy. Nick is coming over later and I want to have something left for him."

"Exercise can actually increase your energy."

"Yeah. Yeah. I know. It won't increase anything on day one of the New-Steph. It's going to kick New-Steph's keister, even at this speed."

"Since you're speaking in third-person, tell the New-Steph she's making excuses not to sweat."

Steph smiled at Jess in the mirror. "See what I have to put up with?"

Elaina expected him to smile back. Instead, he curved an eyebrow.

"She has our best interests in mind." He sounded serious and committed.

"Wow. It didn't take long for her to brainwash you."

"I've let myself go and it's going to take hard work to get back to where I want to be."

"Jess, I intended for Steph to step into my shoes and guide you for a few days while I'm gone. I think YOU should step into them instead and guide her."

Jess's forehead crinkled slightly. "Where are you going?"

Steph rolled her eyes. "To Ohio. Her ex demanded she come get his dog."

The slight crinkle in his forehead deepened. "Demanded?"

"He still tells her to jump, and she asks, 'How high?'"

"Is that true? Does he still call the shots?"

"Steph's leaving out a big chunk of the narrative. Arden will forever TRY to manage me. It's in his blood. He's a huge bosser, who struggles when I tell him to kiss off – something I never did when we were married."

"Given that, why are you heading to Ohio to take his dog?"

"Because Neil is the cutest Pomsky. She has light blue eyes and it looks like she's wearing a black mask."

"Neil's a she?"

"Long story short – Rachel named him after Arden's dad, who was gravely ill at the time. It was a nice gesture on her part. Now that his father is out of immediate danger, Arden wants no part of the dog. He can't handle the early stages of puppy development."

"There's no need to sugar coat his behavior – Arden's, not the dog's." Steph took a swig from her water bottle. "Arden tried to act normal for a very short time to win Rachel. Now that he has her, he's back to his persnickety self."

"Dogs aren't for everyone. I give him credit for trying.

Steph put her finger in her mouth and pretended to gag. "You're way too kind to that jackal."

Jess spoke up. "I get why you go easy on him. Exes are never really out of our lives, even though we have court documents that say they are. In my case, we have a daughter together. Jewel will always be in the background."

"You need a jewel thief to take her off your hands," Steph teased.

A hard gleam glistened in Jess's eyes and Elaina had a hunch some thief did steal Jewel.

"Good one." Jess blotted perspiration from his forehead.

Steph must've realized her attempt at humor failed. "I'm sorry, Jess. Sometimes I can be insensitive. I truly didn't mean to be."

"No harm. No foul."

"Still..."

He put up his hand. "Let's talk about something else. Elaina, could I go with you to Ohio?"

Elaina and Steph exchanged a surprised glance.

"It would give me an opportunity to catch up with Rachel. I haven't seen her in forever. The stiff you were married to won't be happy that I'm there – a huge bonus for you." He winked.

Elaina didn't know whether to grin from ear to ear or decline on the grounds it would be a quick trip there and back. "I can't ask you to delay your music."

"It won't be a problem. I'm always composing in my head."

"I thought you needed quiet."

"I thought so too. Maybe all I needed was a change of scenery." He lifted his shoulders in a shrug. "The vault has been unlocked. The words and notes are flowing like they were never stuck. I wrote several stanzas last night and a few more this morning."

"That's awesome, Jess."

Steph stopped her treadmill. "When you release your next song, we'll tell everyone you composed it here."

"I don't release songs. I sell an album of compositions to a specific artist or group. They add their voices. When they release an album, my part gets released with it."

"I'll still shout from the rafters that the song happened here."

Jess chuckled. "I appreciate that, Steph. Thank you." His gaze returned to Elaina. "Do you mind if I tag along?"

"Umm…" She thought of Chad. He wouldn't be

thrilled with her boarding a plane with Jess, or any man for that matter. They weren't an official couple, but they'd kissed and had intimate conversations a few times. Elaina glanced at Steph and read proceed-with-caution in her expression.

* * *

"You're not Nick." Steph opened the door wider to let Philip come in.

"You're right, I'm not. I'm a lot more handsome."

"You wish." Steph bumped her cheeks up high in an ornery smile and pointed to Philip's shoes. "Off they go."

"Gotcha." He kicked off his boots and placed them on the rubber mat near the door, but left his coat, hat, and wool scarf on.

"Graaaace, you have company."

Grace hustled from the laundry room. "Philip? Hi. I wasn't expecting you."

Philip gathered her in his arms. "I thought I'd surprise you. Would you like to go to dinner?"

"I'd love to." Grace surveyed her appearance in the decorative wall mirror. She fluffed the back of her hair. "Do you mind if I change out of my ratty jeans?"

"Don't change. I dig torn denim."

"You're such a hippy, Philip," Steph quipped from the sideline.

Grace snickered. "She's not wrong, but I 'dig' who you are."

Steph shook her head with amazement. "You two

would've fit perfectly into the flower-power scene fifty years ago."

Philip gave Steph's shoulder a playful push. "Groovy."

The doorbell rang again, sending Steph into a sprint. Disappointment put her tone in a choke hold. "You're also not Nick."

"You are correct, madam. I am not Nick." Chad brushed snow off his coat and stomped his feet on the outside mat before entering. He removed his shoes without being asked and looked around.

"She's on the phone chatting it up with some customers. You're welcome to sneak in and scare the bejesus out of her."

"I'll wait."

Elaina heard the commotion in the living room, but she hadn't finished the call. The folks who'd booked the loft apartment for April was arranging ahead of time for transportation to and from the airport. "You'll arrive on April first at three-twenty in the afternoon. We'll meet you at baggage claim. Look for the Four Sassy Chicks sign. Yes. Thank you. See you then."

Tawny traipsed in and hawk-eyed the reservation ledger. "Woohoo! Guests!"

"Not until April. Annnnd...it's for the loft."

"If Jess is still here, things might get tricky."

"I'm sure he won't have a problem relocating to the main house for a few weeks."

"Steph tells me he's accompanying you to Ohio. What's that about?"

Elaina put a finger to her lips. "Shh."

"Yeah, Chaddy-boy's in the living room. You should probably break it to him gently."

"I don't need his approval."

"So you say."

Elaina kept her response hushed so her voice wouldn't carry, but her steadfastness came through as though she'd hollered. "I don't need anyone's approval."

"Oooo, ouch."

"Chad's been here a few times, but we haven't had an actual date. At Christmastime, he mentioned we should go on one; it hasn't happened. He must be afraid to take me out in public." Elaina chuckled, although she wasn't feeling especially put out by his lack of action and she had yet to drum up the courage to upset that apple cart.

As if on cue, Chad waltzed into the kitchen. "There you are." He smiled at Elaina and gave Tawny a blank stare.

"I can take a hint." Tawny shuffled off.

Chad moved in close. "How've you been?"

"Good." Mmm. He had on earthy cologne that seduced her senses right off the bat. And he looked damned sexy in the uniform.

"Sorry I haven't called or stopped by." He didn't offer a reason.

"No problem. We've been busy getting things ready for an influx of guests."

"You have people coming in this weather?"

"No. But they'll eventually come. Would you like something to drink?"

"Coffee if you have it. I'm officially off the clock, but I'm still in my blues; which means I can't have anything stronger than a cup of joe."

"We always have coffee made in case guests want a cup." Elaina glanced at the clock. In half an hour, she'd have to prepare dinner for Jess. "Speaking of guests, one arrived today. He's taken up residence in the loft out back." She wrenched away from Chad and poured him a mug of coffee. "Do you remember when Rachel called on Thanksgiving to tell me she got engaged to Arden?"

Chad ignored the coffee and put his hands on Elaina's hips. "Vaguely."

Vaguely? How could he not recall the details? It had been a huge deal for her that night. Elaina brought him up to speed. "Rachel was the gal who helped us get even with Arden for being a rat bastard. She stole his newspapers. After a few days he caught her in the act and they fell in love."

"Oh yeah. It's all coming back. Unbelievably weird." Chad blinked slowly, possibly to let her know he wasn't the least bit interested in hearing about Arden or Rachel.

Like it or not, she had to give him the information. "The reason I brought it up is because the guest in our loft happens to be Rachel's cousin."

"Oh."

That was it? No questions?

Chad lowered his head and nuzzled her neck. "You have the softest skin."

"Thank you." Again, Elaina edged away. "Would you like to stay for dinner? I'm making grilled chicken salad, black bean spread, and fresh pears for dessert."

"I can't stay. I just wanted to pop in for a few minutes.

I also wanted to ask if we could do yoga sometime."

"I'd love to. Say when."

"Tomorrow morning before work? Six-ish?"

"I'll be ready."

"Great." He took a few sips of coffee, pecked her on the mouth, and left.

Tawny glided back in. "He came and went faster than you can say handcuffs."

"We're doing yoga bright and early tomorrow."

"Well isn't that special." Mischief rolled off Tawny. "Will he be wearing spandex?"

"I have no idea."

"If you don't mind me saying, Chad is one strange dude; not because he does yoga, but something about him is off. I can't put my finger on what it is though. He seemed so normal at first."

"Tell me about it." Elaina took a package of romaine lettuce from the refrigerator. "It looks like it's going to be you, me, Grace, Philip, and Jess for dinner."

"Count me out. Bart and I texted back and forth while you were in here making googley eyes at Chad. He's taking me to IHOP." Tawny licked her lips. "He knows how to woo a girl. Give me home fries and an omelet, and I'll be his forever. Oh, and I think Grace and Philip are headed out too. So it's just you and our musician friend." Tawny tore off a section of romaine, washed it, and took a bite. "What did Chad say when you told him you and Jess would be taking a trip together?"

"We're not taking a trip together. We'll be rescuing Neil."

"You dodged the question."

"I wasn't in the mood to have to defend my decision. I did tell him that we had a guest."

"You're taking a wait-and-see approach."

She absolutely was; with which guy, she wasn't sure.

* * *

Snowflakes fell lazily from the sky; gliding through the air like feathers. A tiny gap in the clouds allowed the tiniest sliver of moonlight to beam through, making it a tranquil winter's night. Elaina inhaled a breath of cool air, thankful the hellacious wind from earlier died down.

She removed the last bit of snow from the deck and propped the shovel against the house.

"Hey, snow bunny." Jess sauntered up the walk. "Which lovely lady is hidden beneath all those layers?"

"Snow bunny," Elaina repeated. "Good one, Jess."

"Now I know – the one with the voice as warm and sweet as blueberry cobbler fresh from the oven."

Words rushed out of Elaina without any forethought. "How can a girl not melt when a guy references something so delicious?"

Through the small slit in the woolen scarf Elaina had wrapped around her head, she met Jess's eyes. For an extraordinarily long moment, they both seemed to be in a trance.

The thirty-second daze got swept away by a loud ping from a cell phone.

"Ahh. I suspect my daughter has finally answered my

text." Jess emitted a small snicker. "Kids." He raised his palms. "I could get pissy with Alyssa for not replying shortly after she received it. Or I can accept that she's not going to get back with me until she exhausts all conversations with her friends. Which one should I do?"

Elaina almost said, "I wouldn't know." At the last second, she rolled back the comment. When folks realized she didn't have children, she became the recipient of sympathy or was given an odd look. She didn't want either one. Having a child would've been incredible, but it wasn't meant to be. The thought produced a bit of melancholia. She wouldn't let the past mess with tonight. "Tawny's boys have been known to not answer her messages for days. It drives her nuts."

"You have kids?"

"I don't."

The odd look she didn't want to come showed up by way of Jess's hard blink. It was a mix of curiosity and sympathy. His phone pinged a second time. "I want to delay responding to give her a taste of how it feels, but I can't help myself."

"You're dying to talk to her. You should get to it, before the chance goes away." She opened the door and stepped aside for him to enter.

He shook his head. "Ladies first."

"A true gentleman."

"My ex would dispute that claim." Jess wandered into the living room with his phone.

Elaina remained in the kitchen, but an occasional 'Really?' floated into the air, followed by a tender laugh.

She smiled at the easy rapport he seemed to have with his daughter.

Jess peeked around the archway. "It looks and smells great." He noticed the place setting, complete with cloth napkin and snowman napkin ring. "Nice. There's something special about eating at the kitchen table. A lot of days I balance a dish over my keyboard." He looked around. "Will the others be joining us?"

"Not tonight." Elaina placed two salads on the table. "Their men have swept them away for the evening."

Jess pulled her chair out.

"Did your guy pass up an opportunity to do the same thing?"

Elaina modestly cleared her throat. "He stopped by earlier to say hello and to arrange a yoga session for in the morning. You're welcome to join us."

"Thank you, but I'll tell you upfront it won't happen. I'm as limber as a broom. I'd be wise to stick to the treadmill."

"Yoga can make you less broom-like."

"It's supposed to also help with stress. I know about the benefits. I just don't think it's for me."

"I won't pressure you."

He winked. "Look at this thing." Twice he turned the ten inch plate around on the place mat. "This rabbit food could easily feed two people."

"It's a lot. The plan is to keep you full longer, to avoid a late night snack binge." Elaina laced her fingers, bowed her head, and quietly said grace.

With all the gusto of a man eager to fill his empty

belly, Jess stabbed a chunk of grilled chicken from the top of his salad. The fork was almost to his mouth, he paused to give Elaina a brief smile. "Your guy doesn't know what he's missing."

Elaina wouldn't allow herself to assume anything other than he meant Chad was missing out on a good meal. "I love simple food like salads." Forking a carrot curl into her mouth, she chewed and watched him devour several bites. "I'm not sure if you're a fan of black beans, but I found a recipe for a spread that has salsa and a little bit of cottage cheese in it." She hopped up from her chair and took a dish from the refrigerator. Setting it between them, she also put a bowl of blue corn tortilla chips on the table.

"Interesting." He scooped some of the black bean spread onto a small plate and added a few chips. "How did they make these blue?"

"They're made from blue corn."

"I didn't know there was such a thing." Jess dipped a chip into the spread and took a bite. "Tasty."

"The blue chips have anthocyanins, which according to the internet, gives them more protein. They have less starch than light-colored chips." She bumped his hand with hers. "That's your healthy eating information for today."

He held up a chip and studied it. "You're taking great care of me already. My body thanks you."

"I forgot to ask what you'd like to drink."

"Just water."

"Me too." Elaina started to get up from the table again.

Jess jutted a hand in front of her. "You don't have to wait on me. I'll get it for us. So I don't rifle through your cabinets, tell me where you keep your glasses."

"In the farthest cabinet on the right."

With two glasses of ice water, he returned with a smile. "I told you how I came to live in Maine. How did you and the girls end up here?"

Picking a black olive from her salad, she popped it in her mouth. "It's a long story."

Jess glanced at the clock. "Unless you have to be somewhere, we have all night. I'd like to hear."

Elaina drizzled raspberry vinaigrette dressing over her salad. "I'll give you the short version. Steph fell for Jack Kirby, whose family bought this place. They picked up stakes in Ohio and moved here. Steph was ready to follow Jack so they could be together. The Kirbys owned the bed and breakfast for a very short time and must've decided it wasn't what they thought it would be. They put it up for sale and moved to Florida. In the process, Steph's heart got stomped when Jack basically cut her loose." She frowned. "Steph's a sweetheart and deserved better. Anyway, Tawny wasn't happy at the hospital where she worked, thanks to a boss that didn't like her from the moment they met. Grace wasn't thrilled with her job at the bank. And my ex hired someone to stalk and spook me, thinking I'd sell him the house I got in the divorce. He eventually got the house back, but on my terms. So here we are, four sassy chicks who have an enterprise of our own."

"Your ex husband paid someone to stalk you?"

"Not with cash. He promised the son of a close friend an SUV for his stalking services."

Jess called Arden a jackass. "And the kid can't be too bright."

"Actually, Landyn's very intelligent. He just had a weak moment and Arden took advantage. The clunker he drove back and forth to class died and he was in desperate need of a reliable vehicle."

Jess gave her an incredulous look. "Instead of doing a deal with the devil, couldn't he have taken a loan or asked his parents for financial assistance?"

Elaina hedged on throwing Landyn even further under the bus. "They were already helping him pay the exorbitant tuition for school."

"Is he going to be a doctor?"

She muttered, "Lawyer."

Jess's eyebrows shot up.

"The irony, right? Landyn wasn't a smooth criminal. We nabbed him in the act. He was afraid we'd report him and he'd get kicked out of school. We gave him no choice. He had to nark out Arden." She chuckled. "This short version of how we got here gets longer by the second."

"It's obvious you didn't press charges, since Arden is now married to my cousin." He made a face of disgust. "How did Landyn fare?"

"He got his shiny new SUV."

"You're too nice."

"Not really. At the same time the stalking came to an end, everyone's grunge got to be too much and I got a wild idea. I made Arden pay through the nose for my house. I also made him buy my fitness center. With some of the money, the bed and breakfast was purchased. Voila! We're getting a fresh start in The Pine Tree State."

Jess was silent for a minute and he looked deep in thought. "I don't claim to know anything about psychology, but it seems as though people who make a drastic change, don't do it because of their current circumstances. It's more of a quest to rectify something that's laid dormant for a while in their subconscious."

"Our fresh start is to rectify something in our subconscious?" Elaina licked dressing from her lip and contemplated Jess's point of view. "It could be true in my case. I might have subconsciously left Cherry Ridge to find an answer to something I didn't realize I wanted to solve. When I first came to Portland, I happened to see this anchor necklace," she ran her fingertips over the sterling silver anchor, "in a jewelry store window. I usually have to see something a couple times before I decide to buy, but I knew right then I had to have it. In my discussion with the jeweler, he asked if I was a captain's daughter. I told him how my mom decorated our home with nautical-themed items and that she'd constantly talked about her love for the sea. He suggested I find out the reason why it was important to her."

Jess leaned and lifted the charm to inspect the detailed craftsmanship. His fingers brushed her skin ever-so-lightly.

Elaina shivered from his touch. She covered the

reaction with an off-the-cuff remark. "Maybe she was a dolphin in another life."

Sipping from his water glass, he breached the short distance separating them and spoke softly, "You have to find out." He hurried to make clear what he meant. "Not if she was a dolphin, but why water made her happy. You've not mentioned siblings. Am I to assume you're an only child too?"

"I am."

Again, his expression turned reflective. "It's a different kind of life, isn't it? Only someone who's grown up without brothers or sisters understands what I mean."

"My heart has always ached for a sister. I found her in Tawny, Steph, and Grace. I'm sure you wished for a brother."

"A brother or sister, it didn't matter." Jess laid his fork down and switched gears. "Do you like seafood?"

"It's heavenly."

"After we retrieve that tiny pup from the guy who should be behind bars and we get back to Maine, can I take you for a ride up and down the coast? We'll eat lobster and crab, pretend it's summer instead of the dead of winter, and maybe in one of those moments, you'll find the answer you're looking for."

Elaina touched his fingers. "You'd do that for me?"

"It's the least I can do. You're making me eat salad and some kind of funky bean dip."

* * *

Elaina followed Chad into the fitness room and grabbed a pair of yoga mats from the bin near the rowing machine. She tried to keep her gaze averted from the charcoal-colored yoga shorts that stretched across his fabulous bottom. Of course when he turned, there was no way her eyes would stay off his broad chest keenly highlighted by one of those cool-dry compression shirts. Every inch of Officer Chad Ferguson was muscled fineness. In order to achieve that kind of body excellence, he had to have given it his all and to maintain it, spend lots of time in the gym. She wondered if he gave his best to everything he did, including... From out of the blue, came a quiet groan and a reminder it was too early in the day to engage in lusty thoughts. Frankly, she'd rather drool over a mug of coffee with a splash of French vanilla creamer, instead of Chad's manly perfection. *I AM getting old!*

Chad uncurled his mat and assumed a bound angle pose. He extended his legs out and bent his knees. He completed the position by bringing the soles of his feet together. "You're quiet this morning."

She mimicked the pose. "Early morning brain fog due to lack of caffeine."

"You should begin your day with lots of water, not a pot of coffee."

"Bite your tongue, evil man!" Elaina found that ridiculously funny and erupted into snorting laughter. She teetered sideways.

Chad didn't crack a smile.

Elaina straightened. "Right. More water. Less coffee." She wouldn't defend herself; she didn't need to. Every morning, as soon as her feet hit the kitchen floor, she drank two eight-ounce glasses of water. Coffee came next. Lots of it. Was she addicted? Yes. Did she want Chad telling her what to do? No.

"How'd you sleep?"

Elaina stretched her neck from side to side. "Great. You?"

"Barely closed my eyes," he admitted.

"You should drink more water." At his lifted eyebrow, she decided being a smart alek wasn't in her best interest. "Did you take part in a stakeout?"

"I wish."

Most people wished to win the lottery, not to be part of stakeouts. "Were you involved in a high speed chase?"

"In this snow?"

The question didn't require an answer, but she wanted to respond to his condescension by rolling up her mat and hitting him with it.

Chad went into a lotus pose. "There are stupid criminals who try to outrun the law, even when there's a high risk of ending up in a snow drift."

"No stakeout or stupid criminals. What kept you from getting forty winks?"

He squatted to stretch out his hips and lower back.

In the mirror, she could see him avoiding her eyes. "Chad?"

He held the squat pose for a few more seconds and sat down. "My life has taken an abrupt change. For the better. It's no secret that I've always wanted to be part of hostage negotiations and a counterterrorism team. New York City came through with an offer."

That had to be why he'd been acting peculiar the last few weeks. "It was a secret to me. Congratulations."

"Now that they've made an offer, I'm struggling with the fact that if I accept, I'll have to relocate." He brought his knees up, laced his fingers, and propped his elbows on his thighs. "Want to come with me?"

Elaina drew back, gobsmacked. Surely he wasn't serious. Their relationship hadn't developed to the point where she could entertain such a request. "I can't foresee another move."

"I knew that would be your answer and I understand it. I do. You're still adjusting to Maine. Your friends wouldn't be happy if you left." He winced. "The friends I've made on the force will slap me on the back and wish me well, but I'll feel as though I'm letting them down."

"If you don't follow your dream because you fear letting someone down, what you'll actually be doing is letting yourself down. Your true friends will stay your true friends and will continue to encourage you, regardless of the distance. And you'd do the same for them."

"Your ability to put things into perspective is an amazing thing, Elaina." He smiled with his eyes. "It'll be hard for me to walk away."

Now she felt guilty for wanting to whap him with her yoga mat. "Chad, it's okay. Really. I'm one of your many true friends. I'll listen when you need an ear and I'd be delighted to do yoga with you whenever you're in town."

"A guy couldn't ask for more. Thanks, Elaina." He stood and held out his hand. "Let's get a cup of coffee."

"Are you sure you don't want water?"

Chapter Six

- Like a boss! -

"What's up with Grace?" Tawny jammed her hands on her hips. "She's going at the toilets on the third floor like they haven't been scrubbed in years."

"Grace doesn't do toilets." Elaina folded the newspaper and swung her legs to the floor. She'd been curled up in the purple Gothic monstrosity, reading an article about the mystique of Maine.

"Should we be concerned?"

"Not necessarily."

"You always choose the best words. Will you go up and find out what's bugging her?"

"If she wanted to talk, she wouldn't be taking her angst out on bathroom fixtures."

Tawny drew her face into a scowl. "Usually you're all over these situations."

"We don't even know if there is a situation. It might just be an increase in hot flashes making her grouchy." Elaina tossed out a reminder that when they decided to live together, they agreed to give each other space.

"Yeah, yeah, whatever. Think about it. Grace is up to her elbows in toilet cleaner and cussing under her breath – at eight o'clock in the morning. Factor in how clear she made it on move-in day that she'd pull her weight around here, but in no way did she want to be stuck with bathroom detail. There's either something terribly wrong or she's turned into a germ-a-phobe."

"Grace does have some weird hang-ups."

"You're taking this conversation in circles. Was there a full moon last night?" Tawny sighed with resignation. "There had to be. Nothing else explains half of us turning into loons. Steph isn't up yet, so the percentage might climb."

The racket of something being thrown or slammed shut startled them both.

Elaina nodded. "Let's investigate."

In the farthest bathroom, which hadn't been used in weeks, they found Grace on her knees, with a myriad of cleaner at her fingertips. She flinched when she noticed their presence.

Grace's eyes were as red and watery as someone who'd been on a seventy-two hour whisky binge. Elaina spared a brief glance at Tawny and received an I-told-you-so look.

"Grace, you're making enough noise to disturb the mice in the basement."

Instead of Grace reacting to Elaina's cockeyed attempt to get to the heart of things, Tawny did. "We have mice?"

"It was a figure of speech." Elaina knelt on one side of

Grace and Tawny took a spot on the other side. "You're up early."

Tawny expanded on Elaina's lead-in. "And cleaning toilets."

Grace sniffed. "I've been up since four."

"You didn't have to get up in the middle of the night to clean commodes." Elaina knew Grace's early rise had nothing to do with a desire to make bathrooms sparkle.

"Your humor is not appreciated this morning."

Tawny placed a hand on Grace's shoulder. "It's how we roll."

"Well stop rolling and leave me the hell alone."

Cussing, grouchy, and cleaning toilets – something or someone had tilted Grace's axis.

"Did you catch Philip smoking weed?"

Grace's low growl served as a warning to back off. "This has nothing to do with cannabis or Philip. And your constant fascination with marijuana gets on my nerves." Her frustration turned brittle and she broke into tears.

"I don't have a constant fascination with…" At Elaina's subtle head shake, Tawny cut short her defense.

Elaina knew Grace's triggers and this weepy moment had Cody written all over it. She removed the toilet brush from Grace's hand and gently rolled the yellow cleaning gloves down and off her friends' hands. Without another word, she and Tawny wrapped Grace in a hug.

Between blubbering sobs, Grace tried to speak. "He…he's…not…" She hiccupped. "They're not…"

Elaina kissed Grace's temple. Even though Grace

couldn't get her words out, she'd given them enough to piece together what had transpired. Cody, Isabella, and Karina weren't picking up stakes in Italy and planting them in Maine as originally planned. Grace's slight frame wracked with a hard tremble. Elaina wanted to offer comfort, but she wasn't sure there was anything she could say to soothe the hurt. "Just know we're here for you."

Grace's rested her head on Elaina's shoulder. "They've changed their minds. I'm only going to see my son once a year, if I'm lucky."

This was a let-down of epic proportions for Grace. Elaina fought the tears welling in her own eyes. Tawny was having a difficult time too, as evidenced by her repeated sniffing.

Steph peered around the door. "I didn't get home until well after three and you guys are... Why are you on the floor?"

"Not now, Steph!" Tawny quipped like a boss.

Grace raised her head. "My son and his new family are staying in Italy."

"Aww, Grace! That sucks!" Steph joined the huddle and lifted Grace's chin. "Why are you bawling your eyes out? You want him to be happy, don't you?"

Grace reacted to Steph's indelicate attitude with a jerk of her neck. "Owwww!"

Steph stretched her mouth wide with a wince. "Did you just give yourself whiplash?"

Grace glared.

"At least you didn't sprain an ankle this time."

Grace put a hand on her forehead. "I'd forgotten about that particular lack of coordination."

The day Cody called to inform his mom he was getting married, she'd rushed down the stairs to take the call and tumbled down the last few steps, which earned her a trip to the ER.

"You're as big a klutz as I am," Steph said. "But you bawl way more than I do."

"No I don't."

"Yes you do."

Elaina settled the argument. "We all cry. It's a healthy release."

Lula peeked around the wash basin where she'd been taking it all in. Tawny pulled to a stand and the skittish feline ducked back in her hiding place.

"This bathroom is healthy. You cleaned a clean bathroom. How about you take a stab at a dirty one? Mine is in need of your services."

Grace grabbed the yellow gloves and threw them to Tawny. "I don't think so."

Tawny snickered. "It'll improve your mood." She dropped the gloves in Grace's lap. "Get to it. Chop, chop."

"I hate to throw a wrench in all this bossiness, but we are a bed and breakfast. Our one and only guest will show up soon and want breakfast."

The mention of food sprung Steph into action. She bolted out of the room and to the stairs.

"Umm, Steph."

Steph turned. "What now?"

Elaina pointed to her feet. "You might want to reconsider the fuzzy slippers and maybe change out of your lizard pajamas."

"They're geckos."

"Oh, that's right." She loved ribbing Steph.

"Heckler."

"Gecko lover."

The back door opened and closed.

"Good thing we keep bacon fried up ahead of time and muffins baked. I'll start making scrambled eggs."

"Thanks, Elaina. I'll hurry." Steph zipped away.

"Take your time. We don't want YOU to sprain an ankle."

Tawny passed Elaina on the steps. "When we met, you wouldn't mouth off if someone paid you to do it. What happened?"

"You ladies happened and my life will never be the same."

"You're so lucky."

"I know."

* * *

"Here's your made-to-order egg, cheese, green pepper, and extra onion omelet." Tawny placed it in front of Jess. "Elaina made me put those avocado slices and radishes on your plate too." She made a face. "The woman does not know how to do breakfast. Avocados, I can tolerate. Who in their right mind starts the day with radishes?"

He shrugged. "They're supposed to be good for you."

"There are other foods out there – actual *breakfast* foods – that won't tick off your taste buds."

"I can hear you."

"Of course you can. You have dog ears." Tawny dropped a napkin on her lap. "She sees everything too, Jess. I swear she has eyes in the back of her head." As if to test, Tawny stole a radish slice from his plate and popped it in her mouth.

"I saw that."

"You're right, she does." Jess knuckle-bumped Tawny.

Tawny switched gears faster than most people blinked. "Do you get ideas in the shower?"

Elaina had just poured herself a glass of grapefruit juice and almost knocked over the pitcher. She propped against the half-wall that separated the kitchen from the dining area where guests ate their meals.

"What kind of ideas are you referring to?"

"Musical ideas." Tawny followed his lead and put a few splotches of salsa on her omelet. "I've done some research on you."

"Did they expunge that murder rap from my record?"

Tawny did a theatrical lean away.

Jess grinned over the edge of his coffee cup. "I get inspiration from everything. And yes, sometimes it comes in the shower."

Grace traipsed in with a less downtrodden face. "Something smells good."

Tawny didn't miss a beat. "My feet."

Elaina took a seat at the table. "So inappropriate, Tawn'."

Grace patted her on the back. "Stop fighting the chaos and embrace it."

"Are you saying what I think you're saying?"

"I think I am."

"Life at the Four Sassy Chicks Bed and Breakfast is back on an even keel?"

"It totally is."

Elaina was relieved. Grace had come to grips with the fact Cody and his family wouldn't become part of Maine's landscape anytime soon. In the span of an hour, a small bout of hysteria and a good cry must've worked wonders.

Tawny took a slice of rye toast from the platter. "They have their own language, Jess. It's about as easy to understand as Klingon."

Steph came in looking refreshed and happy. "Thank you for making breakfast this morning, Elaina. My butt was dragging, big time. Some days I feel like I'm eighty instead of forty."

"You might need to up your iron," Tawny said between chews of toast.

"Or I need to get to bed at a decent time."

"Yeah, that too."

"I can relate."

All eyes swung to Jess. "When inspiration hits," he winked at Tawny, "I can't go to bed. I have to stay up and get it out of my head and onto the keyboard. If you see a light on in the loft in the middle of the night, you'll know what I'm doing."

"Taking a shower?"

Steph gave Tawny a puzzled look.

Jess and Tawny rapidly raised and lowered their eyebrows at each other.

"You miss a lot when you're the last one at the breakfast table." Elaina passed around the plate of fresh fruit.

"Obviously." Steph picked out a few slices of pineapple and mango, and instead of an omelet, she chose a boiled egg.

Mischief still beamed from Tawny. "Your birthday is rapidly approaching. What should we do to you?"

"You mean, what would I like to do?"

"No. I said it right."

Elaina groaned. "Let's talk about feet."

* * *

Stony raised his head and went into a yowling frenzy. He loped over to the large picture window in the living room, shoved his nose between the curtains, and wagged his tail like he was dusting furniture. When the doorbell rang, Stony was first at the door. As soon as Tawny opened it, he was as all over Bart.

Bart-the-dog-catcher pecked Tawny's cheek with a kiss and crouched so he was eye to eye with the hairy love of her life. He let Stony lick his face. "Have you been taking care of my best gal, Stone-man?"

Stony let out another yowl of delight.

Bart smiled up at Tawny. "I'll take that as a yes." He ran his fingers through the velvet fur on Stony's head and fished a treat from his pocket. "You know the drill."

He made a fist and Stony sat. Bart opened his palm and the pooch placed his paw in it. After a quick shake, Bart held up two fingers and lowered them for Stony to drop down to his belly. "Good boy." The steak-shaped treat was scarfed up in a nano-second. "You've done a great job with him, Tawny."

Tawny wrinkled her nose with a smile. "Now if I could use the same technique on my boys, I'd be all set."

Steph jumped into the conversation. "You'd have better luck using it on Lula."

"You've got that right."

"Missing them?" Bart asked.

"Always."

"As of the first of the year, I have all my vacation hours earned back. We could fly to California and Oregon; or the other way around. I'd love to meet them."

Tawny stubbornly shook her head. "It's their turn to come here. And their turn to text me. They could even pick up the phone once in a while, so I can actually hear their voices. I'm the only one who makes an effort." She made a histrionic moan of pain. "I sound like a broken record."

Bart drew to a stand and spoke in a tender voice. "Since they're so far away, will Stone-man and I suffice?"

Elaina could've sworn Tawny melted on the spot. She gestured for Steph and Grace to follow her out of the living room, to give them privacy.

Grace said she was interested in learning how to snowboard, and if anyone needed her, they could find her in her room scouring YouTube for videos.

Steph intended to search her favorite online recipe site for low-cal dishes to serve with sauerkraut.

Elaina informed them she planned to kill time down by the waterfront.

Grace changed her mind about the videos and asked to go along.

Steph also had a change of heart about being stuck inside.

Elaina tried to sneak by Tawny and Bart to get her coat out of the closet.

Tawny gave her the side-eye.

"Can we take snow dog outside for a while?"

"Umm, that would be great."

Stony took off running and scaled the kitchen gate in one fluid leap.

"Okay then."

Steph's mouth unhinged at the jaw. "Did you see that?"

"Stony showing us who's boss? Or Bart grabbing Tawny's butt?" At Steph's slow-blink of 'really', Grace said she'd seen both.

***

Despite the temperature being in the single digits and mounds of snow as tall as buildings, the sun streaked the sky with brilliant rays, giving the illusion of warmth.

Elaina inhaled a breath of crisp air and stared out at the ocean, feeling a sense of belonging. "Incredible!"

"Incredible my arse. It's freaking freezing out here."

Grace pulled her chunky, crocheted newsboy-type hat down over her ears for the hundredth time. "Whose genius idea was it for us to come out here? Oh yeah," she feigned an annoyed look, but couldn't keep it intact, "it was yours."

"Just so you know, no one twisted your arm to tag along."

Grace stuck out her tongue. "Just so you know, the end of your nose is red."

Steph got in on the action. "Just so you know, you actually have to be outside in the cold to snowboard. Need I say more?"

Grace narrowed her eyes at Steph. "Just so you know, you're in danger of being thrown into a snow drift."

"Just so you know, you don't have the weight to back up your threat."

"Just so you know, this game is getting old. You two can square off, but Stony and I are going to continue our walk." Elaina pointed to a Black Guillemot swimming close to the marina. The magnificent bird with its winter plumage didn't seem to mind the frigid water or the fact some of the inland water had frozen over. "If Stone-man sees him, he'll try to go in after him. Come on, boy, it's time for you to exercise those hairy legs."

The sound of a snow plow scraping snow off a side street, the unique noise made by chains on car tires, and the joyful resonance of children playing outside made Elaina pause and reflect on how the harsh weather conditions didn't bring Maine to a standstill. There were probably days where people hibernated, but today it was business as usual.

Grace hollered a breathy, "Wait."

Elaina glanced back to find Steph bent down and Grace pulling her along. "We don't know them, Stony."

Steph fired back, "Yes you do."

Grace pointed east. "There's a coffee shop two blocks down. Let's get a cup to drink while we explore the neighborhood." She almost lost her balance on a slippery spot. Elaina caught her in the nick of time. "That was a close one. You saved me from making a spectacle of myself."

Elaina snickered. "You already had that covered when Steph used you as a pair of skis."

"Bwahaha. Since you saved me from cracking my skull on the pavement, I have to pretend you're funny."

"Save your fake laughter and buy me a caramel macchiato."

As they walked, Stony sprinkled yellow DNA on just about every snow bank.

At the end of the first block, Grace started another just-so-you-know session, only switched it up to did-you-know. "Did you know Maine is home to gray seals and the seals give birth to their pups sometimes in January, sometimes in February?"

"That tidbit escaped me." Elaina tugged on Stony's leash because he wanted to go left and she wanted to go right.

Steph bumped Grace with her hip. "You're the queen of random. Elaina, remember when she told us what a liger is?"

"It's the offspring of a male lion and female tiger," Grace stated matter-of-factly.

Steph added, "And that Maine used to be part of Massachusetts."

"My head is full of useless knowledge and sometimes it leaks out."

Elaina issued Grace a high-cheek grin. "I love when it does."

"It's about to leak again. Did you know there's a cannery in Wilton that cans dandelions and fiddleheads?"

"Interesting." Under her breath, Elaina said, "Not enough to actually buy a can."

"You know what they say? When in Maine..."

"Eat lobster?" Elaina gave her a goofy grin.

"Do like the Mainiacs do – eat dandelions and fiddleheads." At the crosswalk, Grace pressed the push-to-walk button.

"Care to clue me in to what a fiddlehead might be?"

"It's the frond of a young ostrich fern."

"Would I know a frond, if I saw it? I'm not even sure I know what an ostrich fern is."

"A frond is the curled leaf of the fern. And an ostrich fern..."

Steph put up a hand. "I'll take this one. Ostrich ferns are feathery. They prefer cooler climates, and in uncultivated areas, they can grow as tall as six feet."

Elaina ran her hand the length of Stony's back. "They're bullshitting me, Stone-man."

He blinked.

"See? He agrees."

Grace took Stony's face in her hands and pretended to be a dog-whisperer. "What? You could tell Elaina already knew what an ostrich fern was by the twinkle in her eyes? Then again, Steph was mimicking Siri, so you're not sure." She put her ear to Stony's mouth. "You're saying if Elaina got out more, she'd know about things like ferns and fronds?"

"And you call *me* a dork."

Mischief crinkled the corners of Grace's eyes. "Regarding you getting out more, when is Chad going to take you out to dinner or show you Portland?"

Elaina raised her eyebrows. "You teased me with the mention of coffee and now you're lollygagging by talking to dogs and asking questions I can't answer. I need a caffeine fix in a really big way." She gave Stony more leeway with his leash and he broke into a run. It took speed-walking to keep up with him.

"Steph, see how cunningly she deflected?"

"She's an expert deflector."

They had to wait for the traffic light to turn red.

"You tried to get away, but here we all are with seconds to kill. Again I ask, what's up with Chaddy-boy?"

"Chaddy-boy won't be stopping by anymore."

"Why not?" Grace grabbed a handful of Elaina's coat.

Elaina tugged loose and sprinted across the street with Stony.

* * *

Grace eyed the small piece of luggage in Elaina's hand. "I can't believe after our long discussion about Chad last night, you booked a flight and you're flying out today."

Elaina should at least feel a little down in the dumps that she and Chad weren't going to happen, but she wasn't. The restlessness that had been clawing her from the inside out – the anxiety everyone thought was a midlife crisis – had gone away. She hadn't felt this relaxed in weeks. When Grace said a long discussion, it was an understatement. They kept her up until well after midnight, trying to understand how Chad had been so possessive of Elaina and was now on his way to New York without her. They expected her to fall apart. Steph felt guilty that she and Nick were doing well, as were Tawny and Bart, and Grace and Philip. Elaina reassured them that just because the stars didn't align for her and Chad, they didn't need to worry or feel guilty. "Everything fell into place with the flight. I found a great rate and the weather looks good for flying."

Grace sighed. "You're leaving for god knows how long. Tawny is working evenings, which means she'll be sleeping during the day. Steph has committed to help Nicholas at his restaurant, because a member of his kitchen staff had gall bladder surgery. It's going to be me, Stony, and Lula holding down the fort."

"Grace, fear not," Elaina quipped in a sing-song voice, "it'll be a quick trip there and back."

"Fear not? Good one. I blurt out random stuff, but you're pretty good at tossing around Shakespeare."

"Fear not is from the Bible."

"Shakespeare probably said it too."

"You should find out." Elaina rolled her suitcase to the back door.

Grace placed a hand on Elaina's shoulder. "Sorry for

whining about being here by myself. I can handle it. Just hurry back."

"As far as I can see, the four of us will rendezvous on Wednesday. We'll celebrate with wine."

"We should designate Wednesdays as our official wine club night. If the bed and breakfast gets as busy as we anticipate, we're going to need a sanity night to regroup."

"I doth declare the middle of the week as Wine Club Wednesday."

"Doth? What a goofball!" Grace inclined her head toward the door. "Collect Jess and get to the airport or you'll miss your flight."

Stony stood with his paws on the top of the kitchen gate and gave them his famous yowl.

Using an authoritative tone, Elaina commanded him to get down. "No more jumping over the gate."

He whimpered.

"That's not going to work with me. You're not allowed in the kitchen. Stay down." Elaina hit him with a firm look. "Be good for Grace while I'm gone."

"Oooo, when you get all up in his grill like a boss, you give me goose bumps."

Elaina lifted an eyebrow.

"You'd better get all boss-like with Lula too. She has it in for me, I swear. I had a spiral notebook on my desk and she tore it to bits. We should rename her Shredder."

"Lula, behave."

A meow echoed from under the purple beast of a loveseat.

"She's sassing you."

"Doesn't everyone?"

Chapter Seven

- Slinging the slang! -

Thirty-thousand feet above land, with Jess at her elbow, Elaina was both nervous and tickled.

Out of the clear blue, Jess apologized for shoving his way in. He shifted as much as his seat belt would permit and she did the same, bringing them almost face to face. "You don't know me, Elaina. Not really. Just because I'm related to Rachel, you didn't have to agree to let me come along. You're too nice."

Elaina didn't know what to make of the comment. "I am nice, most of the time. I'm also not a pushover. If I didn't want you to come, I would've said so." She inhaled a short breath and exhaled before adding more. "That wasn't always the case. When I was married, I held my tongue and did everything my husband expected of me, not because I wanted to, but it was easier to play the get-along game. In the process, I lost myself – somewhat. I allowed him to squelch my voice, but inside lurked a rebel with thoughts, ideas, creativity and spunk. Once

Arden broke our marriage, the independent woman he'd held down 24/7, stepped out from the shadows and into the light." To alleviate the awkwardness of such a serious and personal narrative, she scoffed. "Boy did I get carried away or what? You made a simple statement and I went on a rant about my ex. I apologize, Jess."

Jess grinned from ear to ear. "No need to apologize. I've gone through a divorce and know how easily the grunge can erupt when you least expect it. I'm glad you shared, especially the part about stepping into the light to be the person you were all along."

The flight attendant stopped at their row of seats with the beverage cart. "Something to drink?"

"White wine and water, please."

Jess ordered the same. He went to pay for both with his credit card. Elaina tried to move his hand away.

The flight attendant waited patiently for them to resolve the issue.

"I'm not trying to boss you," Jess quietly said near Elaina's ear. "I'd just like to buy you a drink."

Elaina relented.

Jess waited for the attendant to move on and then lifted his glass. He gently hit it against Elaina's. "Thank you for trusting me."

"I didn't say I trusted you."

"Not in those exact words, but you said it."

Elaina feigned confusion. She did trust him, but she wanted to hear how he came to that conclusion.

"By telling me who you no longer are, you also let me know you're not a fool who puts herself in peril by traveling with a guy who showed up at her door in need of a place to rent. You had me thoroughly vetted before we got to the airport, didn't you?"

Instead of feeling and looking sheepish for doing exactly what Jess had guessed, Elaina sat up straighter and hit him with the truth. "You're not only musically-gifted, you've also have a keen intuition." Over the rim of the wine cup, she watched him absorb the information. "After you asked to stay in the loft indefinitely, I made some inquiries. I have to protect my friends and our business. Just so you know, before the girls and I moved in together, I checked them out too."

"That sounds logical to me. I checked out okay?"

"No criminal record and you have an excellent credit rating. And you have amazing blue eyes." She meant to soften the blow of also having his financial standing verified as well, but the spontaneous and flirty comment was a surprise even to her. Embarrassed, Elaina chewed on her bottom lip.

"I have no problem with you checking on anything concerning me, including my eyes. Thanks for the compliment. Yours are pretty spectacular too."

"Gracias." She finished her wine in one swallow.

For the next half hour, they stayed away from any discussion of body parts and talked about Ohio and what Jess remembered from having lived there. He recalled going to Cedar Point Amusement Park on Lake Erie with his cousins one summer and playing Little League baseball in Englewood. He talked about tinkering in the garage with his dad, until his father got a big promotion and moved out of the country.

Elaina asked if he'd recently heard from his father.

"A couple weeks ago we talked for ten minutes." He sighed.

That simple breathy noise said a lot and Elaina wanted to hug him, but she didn't because the flight attendant walked through checking to make sure everyone was still belted in.

"I'm sure you miss him."

"I do sometimes." Jess ran a hand through his hair. "My father flew home for the big things – my high school and college graduations, and my wedding. It would've been nice to have him around for some of the things he considered less important. Because of my dad's absence in my life, I made a pledge to Alyssa to be present in hers."

"She's a very lucky daughter."

Jess bragged that he was good with his hands. At Elaina's cocked eyebrow, he grinned. "In all those years that we lived with my aunt and uncle, they taught me how to plumb, do electrical work, make duct work and install heating and air conditioning systems. They owned an HVAC business until Uncle Jake had a series of heart attacks. Now he takes it easy and Aunt Carol works at the winery. My biggest take away from having spent time with them is the importance of family and how life can turn on a dime. They've always supported my interest in music, but they ingrained in me that a person should have more than one set of skills."

"They sound amazing."

An awkward moment settled in.

"Should you have a leaky faucet or a bad breaker in your electrical box, I'm your man."

The airplane hit a small pocket of turbulence.

Elaina flinched.

Jess patted her knee. "We're fine."

A bigger round of disturbance brought the pilot across the loud speaker. "Sorry about that, folks. We might hit a few more as we approach LaGuardia. Please remain seated with your seat belts in place."

"Distract me from this madness, Jess. Tell me more about you."

"You already know my date of birth, where I went to school, who I took to prom, what brand of after shave I use, and that I wear a size thirteen shoe."

Elaina jiggled with an easy laugh. "Funny man. I do know your date of birth, not much else." She elbowed him. "Size thirteen? Really?"

Another jerk of the plane and the pilot happily announced that should be the last one. He also said they would be landing in twenty minutes.

Jess took his phone from his pocket. "You said you like a variety of music. I do too. My mood, like yours, determines what I listen to." He tapped the music app. Have a peek." He handed her the phone.

Elaina scrolled through the selections. She smiled and pushed her shoulder into his. "You like Elvis?"

"Who doesn't?"

She continued to browse. "Jimi Hendrix, Wolfgang Amadeus Mozart, Michael Jackson, Ozzy Osbourne,

Louis Armstrong, Maroon 5, Iggy Azalea, Imagine Dragons, Prince, Dr. Hook, Frank Sinatra, The Beatles." Elaina couldn't believe how many artists he followed and the number of songs he had downloaded. Her eyes skipped back to one group in particular. "Dr. Hook. I kind of remember them. Didn't a member of the band wear an eye patch?"

A smile the size of Maine spread across Jess's face. "That's them. Some days this is my go-to song." He plugged ear buds into the headphone port and tapped the first song on the album. "Have a listen."

Elaina shoved the ear buds in. Her eyes grew wide at the romantic and sensual lyrics of *A LITTLE BIT MORE*. She placed a hand on her heart. "This song speaks to my soul." She wasn't sure she said it out loud. Giving Jess the side-eye, his big smile said she did in fact utter the words and he'd heard. She listened to the song three more times. "That song is great!"

"I had a feeling you'd love it as much as I do."

"We've only known each other a handful of days, yet somehow you're in tune with me. How is that possible?"

* * *

"We have a situation that requires your special touch." Grace spoke in a low voice.

Elaina pointed to the elaborate two-story Cape Cod home coming into view on the right hand side of the street. "It's where the silver Lexus is parked in the driveway." She went back to her phone conversation.

"What kind of situation?"

"Do you remember the waitress we met in eastern Pennsylvania on our way to Maine?"

"How could I forget Norma? She gave you extra bacon when Tawny kept stealing yours. Bacon aside, I recall a sensitive discussion about relationships. Norma's husband Jethro left her for another woman and she found herself in an unhappy rebound marriage to Maurice, Monty, or Mickey."

"Maury."

"Sorry. My brain hit a snag."

"Welcome to the club," Grace teased. "Anyway, you told her to stop by for a visit sometime." She lowered her voice even more. "An hour ago I answered the door and there she stood, with tears in her eyes and three suitcases stowed beside her."

"Register her as a guest."

"She left Maury and doesn't want to go back home. How should I proceed?"

"Be gentle. Make her comfortable and lend an ear if she wants to talk. We know how dark and scary those early days of being on our own are."

"She hasn't stopped crying."

"Do you want me to talk to her?"

"Would you?"

"It's the reason you called."

"You're brilliant. That's why I love you."

"No need to lay it on thick, I already said I'd speak with her."

The candid comment drew a chuckle from Grace.

Elaina heard a muffled exchange and then a few sniffs. "Elaina?"

"Norma, Grace tells me you've come to stay with us for a while."

"I left him. I left Maury. He wasn't a nice guy."

"You kind of expressed that when we talked in P.A. I'm sorry things didn't work out."

"Me too." Norma went into a rant. "Jethro's deceit made me jump from the frying pan into the fire with Maury. I was so heartbroken and clueless. Maury gave me a thimbleful of attention and I let him sweet-talk me into getting married again too soon." A potent sob that sounded as if it came from her soul, traveled through the phone line. "Jethro was a jerk and I navigated to one even worse. I'm so stupid."

Elaina's heart clenched at Norma's sorrow and self-deprecation. She'd felt those exact same feelings not long ago and it had taken three amazing women to catapult her out of the mire. "You're not stupid. Please don't say that, because it isn't true. People who've been hurt don't always think clearly and fall into a trap. When your heart is in a million pieces and a guy offers tape, you let him in." Norma's continued hiccupped sobs brought tears to Elaina's eyes. "You're with friends now. We don't claim to be experts in recovery, but we've been in your shoes. You're welcome to stay for as long as you like." An idea popped into her head, but she wouldn't put it out there until she made a phone call.

"Thank you for everything." Norma's voice no longer cracked when she spoke and the hiccups stopped.

"Jess and I will be back as soon as we get these puppy theatrics over with."

"I look forward to seeing you again. Uh, your dog just put his nose..."

"Sorry about that. Stony goes right for the goods. Push him away and tell him no."

Norma laughed. "He's a sweet dog. Your cat..." She paused.

"Oh no! Did she scratch you?"

"Nothing of the sort. She made up with me right away. I love her!"

Elaina was dumbfounded. She loved Lula too, but lately the cat misbehaved more than she was good. "She's quite the cat."

"After Grace's warning about her, I can't believe she's in my lap and allowing me to pet her."

"That makes two of us."

* * *

"It's about time!" Arden scowled at Elaina like she was a newspaper carrier who delivered his Wednesday's paper on Saturday. A vein pulsed in his forehead and he stood with his arms crossed. The conversation Elaina had with Norma about exes had set the mood for her encounter with Arden.

"I don't jump when you snap your fingers."

"You said you'd come and get the dog."

"I did and here I am. If you expected me to fly out the same day you strongly urged me to come and get Neil, then you need a reality check. I'm not at your beck and call. If you want something from me, you have to get on your knees and beg." Elaina couldn't believe the last line, but she'd put it out there and wouldn't take it back.

"On my knees? That will never happen."

Elaina had encouraged Jess to remain at the bottom step so Arden wouldn't see him right away. She wanted the element of surprise to work in her favor. "Then don't expect the same from me." She did a half-turn, granting Arden an eyeful of Jess.

Arden's eyelids opened as wide as Elaina had ever had seen them, and for twenty seconds, maybe thirty, the dark-haired, blue-eyed, over-confident, obsessive-compulsive barracuda was speechless. Instead of asking Elaina the inevitable question, he leaned past her and tried to prick Jess with contempt. "Who might you be?" He didn't wait for a reply and placed his displeasure back on her. "Who is he?"

Elaina kept a straight face, but inside she was deliriously giddy. "My assistant." She met Jess's gaze and he nodded with approval.

"Assistant?" Arden mocked with a sarcastic laugh. "I thought you would lie and say lover."

Jess reached for Elaina's hand. "I'm her PERSONAL assistant."

He was playing along, but his touch and suggestive tone brought a smile to Elaina's face and a burst of warmth spiraling through her veins.

Arden's wide open eyelids narrowed right away. "I call bullshit, Elaina. You're too uptight, too structured, too..."

Rachel appeared in the doorway. "Elainaaaa!" She pushed past Arden to circle her with a hug. Over her shoulder, she exclaimed, "Holy freaking amazeballs! Is that you, Jess?"

"Amazeballs? We don't talk like that, Rachel."

Rachel did a swift swivel to her husband. "YOU don't talk like that, but I do."

Arden was twice Rachel's age and their way of expressing themselves didn't quite pair up. Although, in a very miniscule way, Arden was correct. People seldom said amazeballs.

To Elaina's astonishment, Arden backed off. A wacky vision of Rachel telling him to go stand in the corner popped into her head and stirred a belly laugh. She held it at bay to keep Arden from blowing a gasket.

Jess squeezed Rachel in a bear hug and gave her a Dutch rub on the head. "How's it going, Cuz'?"

"*You're* the cousin we sent to Elaina as a bed and breakfast guest?"

Rachel was quick to correct Arden. "We didn't send him. I talked to my aunt and she sent him."

Arden ignored the clarification. "And now you're her PERSONAL assistant?"

Jess and Arden engaged in a stare down.

"Knock it off, you two." Rachel grabbed Arden's stiff arm and he seemed to relax in an instant. Elaina wouldn't have believed it had she not seen it with her own eyes. Rachel's influence over Arden was a modern day miracle. "They came a long way, sweetheart. Step aside. We're going to have coffee and let them get to know Neil."

Under his breath, Arden mumbled. "I paid big money for the darn dog and now you want to get rid of him."

Rachel wanted to get rid of him? That didn't add up to the things Arden had said on the phone.

Rachel led them to the kitchen. "I thought I'd be okay with a dog. As it turns out, I'm not. I tried to love her, I really did."

Elaina put out a feeler. "Did the chewing thing get under your skin?"

"She hasn't chewed on anything for several weeks."

"So there's no need to pull her teeth out?"

Rachel was taken aback. "What? No! Why would you say something so silly?"

"Too much recycled air from the airplane tends to make me goofy." Elaina's gaze did a slow crawl to Arden and she gave him a liar, liar pants on fire look. He dropped his eyes to the floor.

"It's more of a dislike for the hair I find everywhere. You seem to have adjusted to all the shedding Stony does. I thought you wouldn't mind one more furball to deal with. What's a little more hair, right?"

"It was your idea to get rid of Neil?"

"Yes. Why would you think otherwise?" Rachel arched an eyebrow at her husband. "You took the heat?"

He didn't reply.

"Aww," Rachel flung her body into him, "you covered for me." She ran her hands through his every-strand-in-place hair and messed it up. He didn't seem to mind.

Elaina stole Rachel's line, "Holy freaking amazeballs!" She broke into a hearty laugh. "Now I've seen everything."

A series of yips coming from upstairs drew their attention.

"That has to be Neil!"

Arden slid "duh" under Elaina's excitement.

She gave him the stink eye.

Rachel took four mugs from the kitchen cabinet. "Elaina and Jess, why don't you go upstairs and meet her. She's in the kennel at the end of the hall."

"We'd love to." Jess clutched Elaina's hand. "Let's go get our dog."

Our dog?

Jess was a surprise a minute.

Sitting in a wire kennel twenty times bigger than her, Neil jumped around when she saw them.

"Hi, girl," Elaina cooed with as much tenderness as she could. She sat near the kennel cross-legged and stroked Neil's silky coat through the open wire of the cage, allowing the tiny pup to get familiar with her. "I know you're excited. We are too."

The eight-inch tall ball of fur went into an even bigger yipping frenzy.

Jess joined Elaina on the floor and carefully opened the door to let the bundle of energy out. He latched onto Neil's collar to keep those little feet from running away. "You are a pretty one." He looked at Elaina. "And so are you, Neil."

Elaina pecked Jess's cheek with a smooch and did the same to Neil's nose. "We have to change your name, sweet pup. Neil just doesn't suit you." The dog stared up at her from where Jess had her restrained in his lap.

"What shall we call you?"

Neil nipped Jess's hand.

"We could call her Nipper or Yipper."

Elaina wrinkled her nose with amusement. "Or Sammy – short for Samantha."

Jess nodded with approval. "It fits her. Okay, Sammy, let the spoiling begin." He pulled to a stand with Sammy cradled in the crook of his arm and extended a hand to help Elaina up. "Let's keep her new name under wraps until we're out of here. Rach' won't mind, but Arden might cause a scene, since she was named after his father."

"You really are a decent guy, Jess Blakefield."

"And you're quite the woman."

Neil tried to work her way out of Jess's hold. "You're a high-energy pooch, that's for sure."

All the way down the steps, Elaina spoke softly to Neil. "Stony is going to love you. Lula? I'm not so sure how that's going to go. She's a wily cat, who thinks she owns the place. She's bigger than you and I can foresee some cat to dog bullying taking place."

"I've only seen Lula once. She took one look at me and ran for cover under that strange purple loveseat."

"It's one of her many hiding places. I have to admit, she's not a people-friendly feline. She'll let me pet her from time to time, mostly she stays hidden until it's time to eat or get a treat. We'll have to guard Neil from those claws."

When they reached the kitchen, Arden straight-armed them. "Stop right there. You can come in, the dog can't." At Elaina's subsequent wince, he added, "My house, my rules."

"You've been dying to say that, haven't you?"

A churlish grin crimped the corners of his mouth. "Maybe."

Elaina rolled her eyes. "You're such an Arden. I guess having coffee with you and Rachel is out, because we're not taking Neil back to her kennel."

Rachel stepped in front of Arden. "We can make an exception for this one time only." She inclined her head for them to enter. "Have a seat. I want to tell y'all about Neil."

Elaina wouldn't gloat that Rachel circumvented Arden's authority. She wanted to, but it would only prolong the discomfort of being in his presence.

"In all fairness, I have to warn you that Neil is extremely hyper. She packs a ton of oomph in that tiny body. She requires a lot of exercise and mental stimulation. If she gets short-changed on those two things, she gets irritable and aggressive." Rachel slid a look at Arden. "We can't have two babies in the house, now can we?"

Elaina had just taken a sip of coffee and it spurted out of her mouth. It took balls the size of boulders for Rachel to call her husband a baby in front of them.

Arden's face became an accordion of lines, but he didn't go after Rachel. He directed his ire at Elaina. "Real classy!"

Jess came to her defense. "That was uncalled for."

"You're right, it was."

Rachel gave both men the stink eye. "Don't make me tase you boys. I have one of those self-defense tasers in my purse and I'm not afraid to use it." She turned her head so only Elaina could see her smirk. "Ya gotta instill the fear of God in them sometimes."

Arden grumbled something under his breath.

Rachel grabbed her husband's hand and kneaded it with her thumb. "We're expecting in July."

Elaina stopped breathing. "W-what? You're having a baby?" How could that be? The entire time she was married to Arden, he made it abundantly clear that he didn't want children.

"We are. Isn't it exciting?"

It took every ounce of her willpower to paste on a bogus smile. "Yes. Absolutely." The hurt that shot to her heart was worse than anything Arden had ever inflicted. "Congratulations!"

Arden didn't say a word.

Jess smoothed his hand up and down her arm. "We need to get on the road."

Elaina numbly lifted her wrist to look at her watch. "You're right."

"Aww, I was hoping we could catch up, Jess. We almost never see each other. What time is your flight?"

"We decided on the way here that since Neil is so young, she'd be terrified when they stored her in the belly of the plane. We're driving back to Maine."

Actually, they hadn't decided anything of the sort, but Elaina concurred with the fib by bobbing her head.

"In the middle of winter? Are you insane? The farther east you go, the more likely you are to encounter snow."

Elaina didn't want to look at Arden – ever again, but her eyes had a mind of their own. He sat with his gaze downcast and he was picking at his finely manicured fingernails. He knew she was hurt and angry. The sting of tears gathering behind her eyes was almost too much to bear. *Do not cry in front of him. Do not cry. Please do not cry.*

He finally looked up and stunned her even more. "I hope at some point you'll be able to forgive me."

"You and Rachel are good together." She stood abruptly and knocked over her coffee cup in the process. Jess caught the cup before it took a nosedive to the floor.

Elaina hugged Rachel. On her way out of the kitchen, she impulsively kissed the top of Arden's head. "Be a good dad."

* * *

"Rachel's announcement caused you pain." Jess leaned across the console and took Elaina's hand.

"Could you please pull out of their driveway? I can't bear to be here one second longer." Elaina cradled Neil, who didn't seem to mind being in the presence of strangers. The dog was probably grateful to be whisked away.

Jess drove two blocks and turned into a church parking lot. "Talk or scream – whatever helps you deal with the shock."

"If I start screaming, I'm not sure I'll be able to stop." Elaina stroked Neil's fur and choked back tears. "He swore he didn't want children, yet Rachel's pregnant."

"It could've happened by accident."

Elaina was on the verge of hysteria. "It wasn't! Arden would've made sure they didn't slip up!" She inhaled a deep breath and exhaled to calm down. "No, he's on board with the idea."

"I wish there was something I could say to take away the hurt."

She swallowed hard and brushed at the salty emotion that came despite her attempt to hold it back. "Arden and I weren't a good fit, and having kids together would've been a disaster. Becoming a mother wasn't in the Master's plan." A hard sob wracked her frame and cracked her voice. "Arden is happy and content, probably for the first time in his life. Regardless of this tiny setback, I'm happy too."

"It's not a tiny setback, Elaina. You don't have to be strong. Cry until you can't cry anymore. It's the only way to purify your thoughts and your soul."

His words pulled the pin from the dam. Elaina lowered her head, cuddled Neil, and gave into an ugly cry.

She heard Jess sniff a few times.

After what felt like an hour, the rushing river ebbed to just a few drops. She dabbed at her eyes with a tissue and blew her nose. "All better."

"It takes time for a gaping wound to heal."

"This one might need stitches." She looked at the digital clock on the dashboard. "Let's get moving. The sooner we get home, the easier it will be on all of us. Right, Neil?"

Neil looked up at Elaina, stretched her mouth with a yawn, and closed her eyes.

"Would you look at that? She's going to sleep. Step on it, Jess. Maybe we can get to the airport before she wakes."

"We're not going to the airport."

* * *

Tawny, Steph, and Grace had been blowing up her phone all day with text messages. Tawn' complained about a reoccurrence of heartburn. She'd had it off and on for a few months; today it was supposedly worse than ever. Steph griped that her butt was dragging from helping out at the restaurant and when she got home she had to save Norma from Grace's cooking. Like Elaina, Grace didn't have it going on in the kitchen.

Steph got tired of texting and made an actual phone call. "I thought I'd talk to you the old-fashioned way. Can you believe Grace was going to feed Norma store-bought lasagna and butter bread?"

"FYI, you're on speaker."

"Thanks for the warning. I wouldn't want Jess to hear me call Grace a biatch." Steph cackled. "Jess, is Elaina making sure you're eating wholesome food and not store-bought lasagna?"

"She's on a mission to make me healthy. At her insistence, we stopped at a department store in Albany to buy a cooler. Then we shopped for food at a grocery store. She had the woman in the deli make us a small vegetable tray with carrots, celery, radishes, cucumber slices, broccoli crowns, chunks of cauliflower, pepper slices – the whole nine yards."

"How did you get a tray in a cooler?"

"As soon as we got in the car, we destroyed the woman's handiwork and shoved everything into a plastic bag. We have fat-free chicken and turkey for sandwiches, twelve grain bread, a quart of skim milk, and baked potato chips."

"Oh you poor guy!"

"Tell me about it. At the last rest stop, we did calisthenics. We raised a few eyebrows when we did pushups in the snow."

Elaina sat grinning at Jess's description of how things had gone. The tale was accurate, but the inflection in his voice was hilarious.

"We walked Neil back and forth on the walkway in front of the parking lot until we put in a mile."

"Sucks to be you."

"Nah," he said, "it's all good. She's looking out for me and Neil."

"That's our Elaina. I've got to go. Grace is pummeling me with her eyes."

Jess stole Steph's line. "Sucks to be you."

The call ended with a laugh.

Less than five minutes later, Grace texted saying if Steph didn't stop acting like commander-in-chief, there would be hell to pay.

Elaina replied, '*Play nice or you're both grounded.*'

'*Ha. Very funny. I'll quit bugging you now. Hurry back.*'

'*I need to talk to Steph again. Is she still near her phone?*'

'*Gonna ground her?*'

'*LOL No. I have something I need to run by her regarding Norma.*'

It took several paragraphs to explain to Steph her idea. In hindsight, she should've called, it would've been easier. '*Do you think Nick would go for it?*'

Steph replied right away. '*You never cease to amaze me, woman. It's an excellent idea. I'll get right on it.*'

Tawny sent another text too. '*Steph is making succotash. Better get your butt home soon or you'll miss it. It'll be a few more days until the sauerkraut is ready – thank goodness. How do I get red nail polish out of carpet? I'm asking for a friend.*'

'*Tell your friend to Google it.*'

Elaina read each text message to Jess.

"Without you they wouldn't know what to do."

"That's what they'd like me to think. What's actually going on is that they're worried about me."

"You got that from those messages?"

"I've learned to read between the lines."

He pulled the car off the highway and into a truck stop-service center to gas up. "Are they worried because you're with me? Or that we decided to drive back?"

"Probably a little of both. We made the trip from Ohio to Maine a few short months ago. Obstacles popped up along the way. When we finally made it to our destination, we vowed never to drive that far again. Yet here I am, on the same stretch of highway."

"I understand why they'd be leery of the trip. Why they're concerned that we're together has me baffled." In the same breath, he said, "I shouldn't have teased Tawny about that murder rap."

"She knew you were kidding."

"Then what?"

Elaina huffed out a breath. "Chad and I broke up; not that we were actually a couple. We met, he was here for Thanksgiving and Christmas, when he wasn't busy he'd pop in to say hi, and now he's relocating to New York." Neil jumped around in her lap. "I told the girls I'm good with him leaving, they don't believe me. And now I'm making a long trip with you."

Jess stared into her eyes for a long moment. "Are you really good with Chad going away?"

"I am."

"You're a strong woman, Elaina."

"I have my moments of strength. As you're well aware, I've been known to turn into a cry-baby."

"Me too," he teased.

"Jess, thank you for everything."

"No thanks needed. I'm tickled to be in your company." He opened his mouth to say more, but must've thought better of it.

"I could go for something to eat. Some real food. How about you?"

"Thank the Lord! I thought you were going to make me eat picnic food the entire trip. If you like, we can get something here or find someplace fancy."

"We can't do fancy. Neil would freak out in the car by herself. I'd be good with whatever we can find that's portable and less picnic-like." Neil jumped around and turned in a circle. "I think our furry princess is doing a pee dance."

Jess pumped gas and Elaina walked Neil to the far edge

of the parking lot where a small patch of grass separated the business property from a farmer's field. While Neil took care of business, Elaina did calf stretches. When they returned to the car, Jess was doing some stretches too.

"I'm dying for a burger and fries. Do you mind?"

"A burger and fries sound great. I'll crack the whip when we get home."

Jess leaned into her personal space. "I'm not into kinky."

"If not a whip, what ARE you into?"

"Lettuce, tomato, mayonnaise and onion – heavy on the onion."

"Me too."

"You like onion?"

"I do."

"My kind of woman." Jess opened the car door so she and Neil could get in. "You're beautiful, intelligent, you like music by Dr. Hook and you aren't afraid of onion. Where have you been all my life?"

Chapter Eight

- The name game! -

"Norma, how are you?" Elaina would've thrown an arm around her, but she had to restrain Neil.

"Better now." Norma glanced around the living room. "This place is incredible and the help is therapeutic. I've bent Grace's ear so much over the past two days, I'm surprised she doesn't duck down when she sees me."

"Grace is great."

Neil went crazy when Stony ran into the room to greet Elaina.

Stony gave her a yowl, but stopped a few feet short of her and cocked his head.

"Stone-man, meet Neil."

Norma drew back with surprise. "He's wearing a pink collar."

"Neil is a she."

"Oh."

Instead of explaining every time someone questioned the sweet dog's name, it was time to call the pooch something else. She originally thought Samantha – Sammy – fit, but the more she was around Neil, the more she was undecided. For now she'd table the name and see how well Stony and Neil got along. Elaina crouched and let Stony sniff the little dog. She rubbed Stony's head and kissed his snout several times. "You have a new friend, Stone-man. You have to be careful with her, okay?" She hugged him tight. "I've missed you, boy." She put Neil on the floor.

With lightning speed, the Pomsky was by Stony's side, jumping around like she was on a sugar high.

Stony pushed her away with his nose.

Neil came at Stony again and nipped at his ankles. Stone-man put his large paw on the dog.

"Way to show her who's boss."

Lula made a rare public appearance and went down on her hunches.

"Crap. She's going to tear into Neil."

"Nah. She'll be good." Norma pulled a treat from her pocket and lured Lula away from Neil. She scooped the cat up and spoke baby talk to her.

Lula purred like a contented feline.

Elaina was flabbergasted. "Grace said Lula had taken to you. I couldn't imagine that wily cat making friends with anyone. But there she is all docile and not making a nuisance of herself."

"I love cats. They're so..."

Tawny came in and finished Norma's comment, "Sneaky? When your back is turned, they become shredders – first Grace's notebook and now my magazine." She held up what was left of her monthly nursing magazine. "There was potting soil on my desk where my ficus sets. It doesn't look as if she's been chewing on the leaves, but I'm fairly certain she's been playing in the dirt."

"They don't get you, Lula."

"You wouldn't want permanent ownership of that precious cat, would you?"

Elaina detected a trace of seriousness in Tawny's question.

"I'd love to have her, but she's part of your family."

"She's a family member that's going to get a swat the next time she destroys anything of mine."

Steph did a lively bounce into the room. "Welcome home, weary traveler. I saved you some succotash."

"You're the best." Elaina was exhausted from having driven straight through, with just a few stops in between to eat and get the circulation going. She'd suggested they check into a motel, but Jess said he was okay to keep driving. He let her drive for a short time when they crossed into Vermont. After a three hour nap, he took the wheel again and didn't relinquish it until they pulled into the driveway of the bed and breakfast. "Will you watch Neil while Jess and I return the rental car?"

"I can follow him, Elaina. You have to be dead-tired."

"That's okay, Steph. It won't take long. We'll be back in half an hour to feast on succotash."

"Are you sure? It's not a problem."

"Thanks for the offer. Please just babysit Neil."

"You got it." Steph dropped to her knees, ran her

hands all over Stony, and then picked up Neil. "Aww, what a cutie!"

Elaina gave Steph big points for giving Stony attention first.

"By the way, did you get a chance to speak with Nick?"

"I did. As soon as you get back, we need to have a brief meeting."

Elaina let out a lengthy yawn. "I'm not sure I'll be able to stay awake."

"I do believe what I have to say will keep your eyes open for a while."

If Elaina had more oomph, she'd quiz Steph for more information. "I'll be back soon."

In the garage, she found Jess running the hand vacuum over the cloth seats of the rental car. Elaina had planned on doing it, but he beat her to it.

"You're a good man, Jess Blakefield."

He shut the vacuum off and hung it on the hook close to the rakes and shovels. "Why thank you, Elaina Samuels."

He looked around. "Where's the tiny furball?"

"Neil has been placed in trusty hands."

"Excellent."

Elaina fished the keys for her SUV out of her purse. "I'll be right behind you." She stepped toward her vehicle.

Jess caught her arm and swung her around and into his chest. "I've wanted to do this from the moment I met you." He planted a hungry kiss on her mouth.

It took a millisecond for her to process the shock. When it passed, she kissed him back with everything she had.

In the dim light of the garage, they parted and stared at one another without speaking.

Finally, Jess asked if he overstepped.

Dazed, Elaina slowly moved her head back and forth. "You did not." She wet her lips with her tongue. "This might be lack of sleep talking, but when we're rested up, will you do it again?"

Jess ran his thumb along her jaw line. "I'm not going to wait." He lifted her chin so they were eye to eye and he gave her another toe-curling kiss.

* * *

Elaina reached for the knob to the back door at the same time the door was flung open.

Steph stood grinning. "Ready to talk?"

"Can it wait until after Jess and I get something to eat? We ate a breakfast burrito," she looked at her watch, "around six this morning and snacked on carrots the rest of the day. We're ready to eat everything in the refrigerator."

Steph looked around Elaina. "I don't see him."

"He'll be here in a few minutes. Alyssa called when we pulled into the garage."

Tawny came to them with Neil against her chest. "She's been whimpering since you left."

Elaina took the bundle of fluff. "Hey, sweet girl."

"Was it love at first sight?" Tawny asked.

"The instant I saw her, I was a goner. Look at her, how could I not fall in love?"

"I wasn't talking about the dog."

Elaina moved from the breezeway into the kitchen.

"I peeked through the window of the door earlier. I saw hot lips make his move."

"Nosy."

"Yes I am. Now dish."

Elaina disregarded Tawny's attempt to wrangle the details. "Steph, you wanted to have a brief meeting. Start talking."

Tawny wagged a finger. "Oh no you don't. You're not going to stiff me on this. You always want the particulars of our relationships, yet when it comes to your own you clam up."

"He's a fabulous kisser. Okay? Steph, proceed."

"Steph, do not proceed. Did you sleep with him?"

Elaina almost choked on a breath of air. "No."

Tawny got in her face. "Why not?"

"An opportunity didn't present itself."

"Again, why not? You had a few thousand miles to make it happen."

"He insisted we keep driving."

"What a bonehead! He's obviously into you. All that heat you two generated in the garage melted the snow on the roof."

Elaina rebalanced Neil to keep her from climbing over her shoulder. "It did not."

"So you agree you generated a phenomenal amount of heat."

They stopped talking when they heard Jess approach. He was humming.

"Hey, ladies. How's it going?

"Good. Good," Tawny repeated. "How are things with you?" The thespian tone in her voice made Jess laugh.

"They think we're crazy for driving straight through."

Jess shrugged at Tawny. "Elaina missed you."

"That's your reason?"

"That's my story and I'm sticking to it."

Elaina handed Neil to Tawny and looped her arm through Jess's. "Let's raid the 'fridge."

Mischief danced across Tawny's face. "There's baked chicken, cheesy potatoes, succotash, and a serving of Elaina that's waiting to be *devoured*."

"You are so going to get it, Westerfield," Elaina muttered quietly.

Grace and Norma made an appearance.

Jess acknowledged each with a nod. "Do you mind if I take my food to the loft?"

"Not at all. Your poor ears need a rest from gabby." Tawny used her hand to mimic talking. "Yak, yak, yak. She's a talker."

"Ease up, Tawn'."

"As soon as I'm finished eating, I'm going to conk out. Don't be alarmed if you don't see me for days – I'm that tired."

"We won't bother you. You need a break from..." Tawny jerked her thumb to Elaina.

"You're trying really hard to get on my last nerve."

Grace intervened. "She's trying to wear you both down to get information. Tawn', head out to the sunroom. As soon as Elaina says goodnight to Jess, Steph wants to say a few words." She laughed her way out of the kitchen.

Tawny whispered, "Sorry," and made herself scarce.

"Forgive those yahoos, Jess. They're worried something is happening between you and me. At the same time, they want us to hook up. I have strange friends."

"You're lucky to have such great friends."

Elaina was frustrated with Tawny, happy and dazed by Jess's kisses, and so tired she could drop where she stood.

* * *

Steph used a pen as a pretend gavel. She hit the glass table several times to get their attention. "I call this meeting to order."

Elaina rested her head against the high-back wicker chair. Her eyelids were on the way closed when Steph ordered her to stay awake.

"This is important. I promise to only take ten minutes of your time."

Elaina barely got "Okay" out and she must've closed her eyes again.

Grace kicked her chair. "Seriously, you'll want to hear this."

Send me an email. I'll read it in the morning.

"As you know, I've not had the best luck with men." Steph paused as though she was waiting for everyone to agree.

"Hurry up, Mathews. We're losing Samuels."

"I'm trying to find the right words."

"Find them all ready," Elaina said testily.

"Nick is excited to hire Norma. I told him we know firsthand that she's an excellent waitress." Again, she paused. It was so not like Steph to throw a break in the conversation.

"Yay," Elaina said with forced enthusiasm. "I hope Norma jumps on the opportunity."

"Do you want to present the offer to her since it was your idea?"

"You can do the honors." Elaina yawned so deep it felt like she dislocated a rib. She adjusted her torso and started to get up.

Grace gave her a gentle push back down. "Lots more to come."

"Please don't say lots."

"Steph, talk fast," Grace urged.

"Nick and I have been working on the cookbook as time permits. With him putting in long hours at the restaurant and me working here, we're not getting much accomplished. He lives across town. That eats up a lot of time too."

Elaina's tired brain could still put two and two together. "You're moving in with Nick."

Steph laughed nervously. "That's not it."

Elaina gathered herself into a semi-fetal position and closed her eyes. "Sorry. I'm down for the count."

Tawny patted Elaina's cheeks. "Not yet, sleeping beauty."

"Keeping me awake is torture."

"There's a group decision to be made and you're part of the group," Grace said. "Steph has been dying to ask you something all day."

"Steph, I love you, and I'm truly interested in anything you want to tell me, but hurry. Please! Say what you have to say right now or I'm headed upstairs."

"Nick knows Lula is being a pain and that she got us that one star review. When I told him that Lula took to Norma like a hummingbird to sugar, an idea popped in his head. His condo allows pets. He thought he and Norma could trade living space. She'd take his condo and he'd move in here...with me."

"He would do that?"

"He's pretty great, right?"

"Indeed. Now can I go to bed?"

"Do we have your blessing?"

"A hundred times yes, but you don't need it. Do I have to beat that concept into you?"

Tawny spoke in a quiet voice. "Even though we annoy you to the point you want to hit us with a hammer, we respect you and what you've done for us. That's why we want to run important things by you first."

"Aww." Elaina was too exhausted to expand on the thought

Grace extended a hand to help her up. "Now you can sleep."

Elaina blurted, "Bailey."

Grace's forehead creased with confusion. "The liqueur?"

"Neil's new name."

"And you call me random."

Elaina was almost out of the sun room. "Arden and Rachel are expecting."

"A package?"

"A baby."

"No wonder you're cranky."

She slurred her words. "I'm not cranky, I'm ecstatic. Can't you tell? I'm also too tired to care."

Chapter Nine

- Topless and sassy! -

Elaina heard the basement door open and close. "I've only been asleep for," she opened an eye to see the amber digits on her clock-radio, "twelve hours?"

"Are you alive?"

"I'm not sure. I hear a voice. At least I think I do."

"Can I turn on a light? I'm afraid I'll bump into something." Elaina's bedroom was located in the far room of the basement. Tawny had flicked on the light to descend the stairs, but it wasn't enough illumination to guide her to where Elaina lay with the comforter shoved up to her nose.

"Sure. I slept longer than I intended." Elaina sat up, stretched, and propped against the headboard.

"I'd still be asleep. Driving that far without a real break, takes a lot out of a person."

"I agree. In hindsight, we should've stopped. The next time I make a trip to Ohio, I'll break up the drive in increments of six to eight hours."

Tawny plopped down on the bed and crawled beside Elaina. "We have to go there as soon as possible."

"I just got back."

"I know, but there's a bit of payback that needs to happen."

Elaina sighed. She knew where Tawny was headed with this. "I don't seek revenge."

Tawny bumped Elaina with her shoulder. "If you don't, you'll stew for the next thirty years."

"No I won't."

"How could he get her pregnant?"

"You have two kids. You know how it's done."

"I wasn't speaking anatomically."

"Tawn', I really don't want to talk about the barracuda. My eyes still hurt from all the crying I did after we left his house."

"You actually allowed yourself to cry?"

"Water poured out of my eyes."

"What did Jess think about it?"

"He got teary-eyed too."

"Because you wouldn't stop blubbering?" Tawny chuckled lightly. "I'm kidding. Of course, he got misty-eyed. It's hard to see someone in that kind of pain. I think he's into you, Elaina. I'll bet the reason he didn't stop driving is he wanted to get you back to your comfort zone."

"I can't absorb it all. My head feels like it's full of circus peanuts."

"Clever. You slid circus in there. This IS your circus and we ARE your monkeys."

"Whatever." Elaina pushed Tawny's leg with her foot. "There's more on your mind than babies, Jess, and monkeys."

"No there isn't. I just missed you."

"I wasn't gone for a week."

"You're the circus trainer. Whenever you're missing in action, the animals go haywire."

"You're not talking about Stony and Lula. It wasn't Steph or Grace either. You're talking about you. What's on your mind Tawny Pia?"

Tawny groaned. "I may have seasonal affective disorder."

"Really?"

"My energy level has tanked and I'm in the mood to bite heads off."

"S.A.D. is a type of depression. Maybe you should schedule a session with a therapist. I'd be happy to go along with you."

"I'm not ready to see a therapist and I'm not depressed."

"You shouldn't self-diagnose, Tawn'. A therapist is trained to identify what's going on. They can suggest ways to pull you out of your funk." Elaina shifted to get comfortable. "I'm going to put some things out there. You can tell me to take a flying leap, if I'm off the mark."

"I'd never do that."

"Yes you would and I'd expect you to. Okay, here goes. I was in a funk shortly after the New Year. You blamed it on a midlife crisis."

"I'm not having a midlife crisis."

"I didn't say you were. I'm just lining up the possibilities." Elaina rubbed the tight muscles at the base of her neck. "Your boys' lack of communication from time to time throws you out of whack. Perhaps Bart is part of the problem. You like your guy to be touchy feely. Bart occasionally grabs hold of you, but mostly he doesn't. How about the hospital scene? Is there someone there that resembles your old boss and her gnarly ways of conducting business?"

"None of the above. Bo and Quentin have taken turns texting me over the past two days. Granted, they're messages are one sentence, but I'll take it. They're buttheads who love me and I've accepted that I rank tenth on their list of people they need to communicate with on a monthly basis. Bart is a great guy. He's sweet and kind, and some days he lights my fire; other days, not so much. I can't foresee him and I for all eternity." Tawny sifted air through her teeth. "You're the only one I've shared that with."

"Thank you for telling me. Your secret is safe until you decide you don't want it to be."

"Regarding the hospital, the people I work with are awesome. There aren't any grouchy bosses who try to make my life a living hell, just nice folks who want to do a good job and go home. So see? I actually may have S.A.D. I should buy one of those Himalayan salt lamps. The pink ones imitate the warm glow of sunshine and are supposed to calm anxiety."

"I have one more thing for you to consider. Tawn', each one of us seems to be going in a different direction these days. Steph and Nick are hitting the ball out of the park with their relationship. Grace and Philip are two crazy birds who just might be in love. And you saw Jess kiss me. Your symptoms could stem from a subconscious fear that if things go well for us, we'll leave you behind."

"Not even close."

"Then buy the lamp."

* * *

"Woohoo!" Steph did the Macarena without music.

"Excessive noise! Stop all ready!" Tawny fled out the back door.

"Why is she so crabby?"

"She's trying to decide what kind of salt lamp to buy." It was a lame reply, but she wouldn't share what Tawny had said in confidence. "You're boiling over with happy this morning. Did Norma agree to trade places with Nick?"

"She's on board with everything. Life is good. Actually, it's better than good. Nick and I will be together more, and that bunch of unfinished papers taking up desk space will become a cookbook in the near future."

"Awesome, Steph! Your year is off to a great start."

"Our little enterprise here is off to a great start too. I took a call a little bit ago from Marcy in Georgia. She and her husband are celebrating their thirtieth wedding anniversary and they're bringing their wedding party along. The reservation is for ten. They'll arrive on the thirteenth and leave a week later. Their plan is to visit as many seafood and crab places as they can and check out ski resorts. I told them I'd have a map ready for them that shows all the resorts in Maine. They also asked about wineries close by."

Elaina imitated Steph with, "Woohoo!" She also did the Macarena sans music.

Grace leaned over the banister. "Do we have guests coming?"

"Uh huh." Elaina flipped into her leader role. "Steph, work your magic. Find some recipes you can prepare ahead of time and make a list of things you'll need. I'll make a trip to the supermarket. Grace, will you vacuum and mop? When Tawny returns, she gets to de-hair the furniture. After I shop, I'll fuel up the van and clean the sidewalks. This place will soon be bursting at the seams with people."

"Take a breath. We have a few days to prepare." Grace ambled down the stairs. "Did Tawny get called into work?"

"No. She bit my head off and stomped outside."

"Tell me about it. I folded towels earlier and there were two pair of underwear in the load. I thought they were hers and took them to her room. She let me know in hurry they weren't hers and threw them at me. She's been PMS'ing all over the place."

"Or heartburn's the culprit. It might be eating a hole in her esophagus."

Elaina put a hand on her throat. "That's a grisly vision I didn't need first thing in the morning."

Grace tugged Elaina into the kitchen by her shirt sleeve. "Coffee is made."

"Ahhh." Elaina inhaled a big whiff. "Nothing like the smell of java to wake the senses."

"I thought Steph woke them with the esophagus thing."

Steph cackled. "I like the shock effect."

"I'm supposed to tell you that Philip wants to paint you for your birthday. Clothing is optional."

Elaina's hand shook when she laughed and coffee from her cup danced over the rim.

"Philip obviously enjoys the shock effect too," Steph seemed happy to point out.

"I'm not shocked that Philip wants to paint me, or anyone, in the buff." Elaina grabbed the roll of paper towels from the counter and began sopping up the mess that now dripped down the front of the cabinet and onto the floor. Something glittered from the corner where the lower cabinets met. "What is this?" She placed the sparkly object in her palm and held it to the light. "It's a teardrop-shaped diamond." She handed it to Grace. "I have to find Tawn'."

Grace asked Steph if any of this made sense to her.

"Nothing ever does."

Elaina pulled on her coat and hat and snatched her phone from the charger.

* * *

"Where are you? I've circled the block twice."

"On the porch."

"I'm looking at the porch. You're not there."

"It's a wrap-around porch. I'm on the section not hit by the wind."

"You had to see me go around two times."

"I thought you were giving your legs some exercise."

"Yeah, right. Stony usually yowls when he sees me. I didn't hear a peep out of him."

"I might've held his mouth closed."

"That's seriously messed up." Elaina growled into the phone and disconnected the call. On the first step to the porch, her foot caught an icy spot. She flailed her arms in an attempt to stay upright.

Tawny rushed to the rescue, with Stony close behind. Their timing was off by a second.

Elaina's keister kissed the sidewalk.

Stony whimpered.

"That had to hurt."

"Ya think?"

Tawny helped her up and returned to the porch with Stone-man. She sat in the rocker with her head down.

Elaina rubbed her backside. With careful movements, she made her way up the steps and across the porch. She took a seat across from Tawny. "You really are a sad little chicken."

"I said as much."

Elaina kicked her heels together to dislodge the remaining snow from the tread on her boots. "Does some of your gloom have anything to do with your wedding ring missing its rock?"

"You went into my room?"

Elaina became aware of her friends' red-rimmed

eyes. She wanted to go over and envelop her in a hug. Given Tawny's irritable frame of mind, she stayed put. "I didn't."

Suspicion swam in Tawny's eyes. "It's the only way you could've known about the setting. I laid the ring on the dresser."

"Again, I did not go into your room. For the record though, we go into each other's rooms all the time. Why are you suddenly being territorial? Are you hiding a stash of weed in there?"

A small smile cracked the tight hold Tawny had on her mouth. "No weed. Not today anyway. Tomorrow might be a different story."

"Just scratch that itch and get it over with." Elaina stretched her foot out and tapped Tawny's boot with hers. "Recreational marijuana is legal in Maine."

Tawny bunched her shoulders in a shrug. "I'm not actually going to indulge. I just like talking about it. Besides, I'm still fighting my tobacco demons. If I light up a doobie, I'll be back to square one." She frowned. "How did we go from talking about my ring to weed?"

Elaina ran her fingers through Stony's coat. "We're weird like that." She'd almost forgotten about Tawny trying to kick the habit, because she wasn't stepping outside as often to smoke. "Where'd they come up with the name doobie?"

"It was the sixties. They said a lot of strange stuff like 'Can you dig it?' and 'Far out!'"

Elaina tossed one into the mix, "Having a gas, meant having fun." The wind changed directions and a powerful gust barreled in, making her shiver. "I came in search of you because… " She paused to let Tawny fill in the blank.

"You found my diamond?"

Elaina did a slow nod.

Tawny tilted her head back and looked up. "Thank you, Jesus!" She was out of her chair in a blink and wrenched an arm snuggly around Elaina. "Thank you. Thank you. Thank you!"

"Is that the real reason you were upset?"

"I may have some S.A.D. or claustrophobia going on too, hence sitting outside freezing in this beastly weather. I should've worn more layers." Tawny's distress turned liquid and formed rivulets down her cheeks. "When we met at that cash for gold event, we were there to trade in our rings. They were a raw reminder that things did not end well. You know the story. We drank wine across the street from the jewelry store and kept the rings. Then we decided to cash them in to fund our trip to Cody's wedding in Italy. At the last minute, you talked us out of it and funded the entire getaway. Grace is the only one who no longer has hers. They're still in her family, only on a different finger – Isabella's." She puffed out her cheeks. "Yesterday I was feeling blue and took the ring out of my jewelry box. I slid it on my finger. When I washed a few dishes by hand, the prongs caught on the dish cloth. The diamond was gone. I went into a heavy panic and thought I was going to throw up."

"I understand. I truly do. Arden has angered me so many times that I've contemplated throwing my ring in the Atlantic or down the sewer. I couldn't follow through with it. Maybe we can't part with the rings because it would close that chapter of our lives forever, and deep down, we still care about those pains in the neck, even though they don't deserve it." She put a finger across her lips. "Shh. Don't tell Arden. He'd find a way to use that information to his advantage." Elaina stood. "Come on, woman. We have a ring to fix, chores to do, and wine to drink."

"Is the wine to help us cope with what you just said?"

"Nope. Wednesday's is a good day to drink fermented grapes. 'Nuff said."

* * *

"Hold still." Philip walked to where Grace sat on the purple loveseat with her chin lifted and shoulders back.

"I didn't go to modeling school. I don't know how to hold a pose for an hour."

"You've been there for two minutes max."

"It feels like an hour."

Grace was giving Philip fits. He moved the loose neckline of Grace's shirt to expose her shoulder. She pulled it back in place.

"You're beautiful. Don't be afraid to show some skin."

"It's the middle of winter and I'm ghostly white. Who wants to see that? Not me."

"You're your own critic. Tanned bodies are nice, but so are ones with natural, creamy skin."

"Lay it on thick, Philip." Tawny plopped down on the sofa with a stalk of celery. She bit into it with a dramatic chomp.

Philip turned and gave Tawn' the really-look.

"Whaaat?"

Elaina answered before Philip. "In order to create something incredible, you need an artistic atmosphere. The sound of celery being demolished by your incisors isn't helpful."

Grace split a gut laughing.

Philip threw up his hands.

Tawny hopped off the couch. "Relax, Michelangelo. I'm going to my room."

"I'll go with."

"It may be S.A.D. or a case of OCD messing with me, but you and everyone else who takes a shortcut when you speak is driving me wonky. 'I'll go with.' That doesn't cut it for me."

Elaina poked her in the ribs. "I'll go with you."

"Better."

"You mean, 'That is so much better.'"

Tawny used her middle finger to scratch her cheek.

"Don't go far, Elaina. Once I get the basic outline for Grace, I want to start working on your painting." He gestured to her black satin blouse. "That's elegant, but severe at the same time. Could you find something easier on the eyes; something with a lot less coverage?" He walked from his easel to where she stood in the middle of the room. "I envision you sitting on the purple beast with just..."

Tawny mouthed off. "It's a birthday picture. She should wear her birthday suit."

***

"Ahhh, the sweet sound of quiet! No madcap painters telling us to bring up our chins or tilt our heads. That was one wild art session." Grace sat four bottles of wine on the kitchen counter. "Blackberry wine for Elaina. Dry red for Tawny. Sangria for Steph. And white Merlot for me."

Steph rummaged through the utensils drawer to get the corkscrew. "You remembered the exact wine we ordered the day we met."

"I have an eidetic memory…sometimes. I'll remember every detail about that day for as long as I live. It ranks near the top of my Best Days Ever list."

"You keep an actual list?"

Grace tapped her forehead. "Up here."

"We should each keep a journal," Tawny suggested. "When we're old and grey, we could supplement our Social Security by co-authoring a book about the four of us."

"No one would believe any of it." Elaina drilled the corkscrew into the cork. "And do not mention Social Security. I don't want to think that far into the future."

"Tomorrow you'll be a year older. Just saying."

"Bite me, Tawn'."

Steph steered them away from age and back to the painting session. "I'm still in awe of how you flipped the channels on Philip. Instead of a birthday portrait of you, he painted the four of us without a stitch on."

Elaina took a big drink of blackberry heaven and

smacked her lips. "We were fully clothed from the waist down."

Tawny opened her bottle of dry red. "We need to give the painting a name; something unusual to make it sound like a priceless work of art. People will come from far away to see it."

"I've got an idea." Grace's light blue eyes gleamed with mischief. "You know that replica of Picasso's *Les Demoiselles d' Avignon* Philip has hanging in the foyer of his studio? Well, we imitated it today. Sort of. Let's call ours *Demoiselles Topless and Sassy.*"

"To jog that eidetic memory you claim to have, *Les Demoiselles d' Avignon* is nude women in a brothel."

"What's your point?"

"For starters, we're not hookers." Elaina advised them to wait and see how the painting turned out and then they could name it. "I can't believe Philip talked us into ditching our bras and covering out chests with a yard or so of lace." She snickered. "We may have to go with *Les Vilaines Filles du Maine.*"

"Translate please." Steph took a big glug of wine.

Elaina waited until Steph swallowed so she wouldn't be sprayed with Sangria. "*The Naughty Girls of Maine.*"

Tawny laughed so hard she snorted. "Grace wanted to be naughty. She got her wish."

"When we actually collect Social Security, we should commemorate the milestone by having Philip paint us again. We'll have him pose us the same way. The name of that painting will be called *Les Vilaines Vilelles dames du Maine,*" Grace spouted.

Steph tapped her glass. "Is that French for wrinkled?"

Elaina jumped in. "It means The Naughty *Old* Ladies of Maine." She teasingly groaned. "I feel ten years older just talking about it."

"How did you ladies get fluent in French all the sudden?"

"It's called Google Translate. I've had my phone in my lap the whole time." Elaina held it up. Grace did the same thing.

"Oh, you guys. You're slick at making yourself sound brilliant."

"That's because we are brill'." Grace stretched out the space in front of her with her hands. "I can see it now. Our risqué painting hanging above the purple beast will make our guests tilt their heads to admire it."

"Or they'll laugh out loud." Elaina hit her finger on the edge of the table to get Grace's full attention. "Strange how Philip had lace in his car. What other props does he keep handy?"

Chapter Ten

~ *Moving on!* ~

Norma fidgeted so much at the breakfast table, Elaina half-expected her to back out of the plan to move into Nick's condo. "Are you okay, Norma?"

"Yes. Mostly." Norma went to squirt maple syrup on her pancakes and missed. A glob landed on a decorative canning jar that contained cinnamon sticks, dried cranberries, and a sprig of evergreen. "Oops."

"Not a problem." Elaina grabbed a wet dish cloth and made the winter centerpiece new again.

"I'm glad it's just the two of us. I need to run something by you."

At the moment, they were alone, but at any second one of the others could wander in. Steph was upstairs, probably on the phone with Nick. Tawny said she was hitting the shower. Grace had yet to make an appearance. Jess had slipped into the kitchen earlier, just long enough to get a wedge of broccoli and cheese quiche, a serving of red raspberries, and one slice of marbled rye toast. He apologized for his absence over the last two days, saying things were going well with his music. "I'm all ears."

This time Norma did a careful drizzle with the syrup, keeping the pour spout an inch from the pancakes. "I have a hard question to ask."

Elaina moved her coffee cup around on her placemat. "The best way to approach a difficult question is to take a confident breath and go for it."

Norma inhaled and exhaled, but she still hesitated. "I don't want to cause problems. Everyone has been so nice to me."

"You're not just a guest at our bed and breakfast, you're also our friend."

"I'm so grateful for your friendship. Without you four ladies, I'd still be in Pennsylvania and stuck in a loveless marriage. It appeared we met by chance, but I'd like to believe you were Heaven sent."

Elaina went all gooey inside. "I don't know if we're Heaven sent, but our paths were meant to cross."

"Which is why putting my question out there is even more daunting. I don't want to mess up a good thing."

Norma's anxiety appeared to be escalating. She repeatedly folded and unfolded her hands, and moved around in her chair so much she could've taken off the varnish.

"I'm going to help you through this. Are you having second thoughts about trading living quarters with Nick?"

Norma's eyelids flared open with surprise. "What? No! I..." She started again. "I know how attached everyone is to Lula, but she and I have a special connection too. It would help me adapt to my new place if she could come stay with me for a while."

Lula was indeed part of the family, in a particularly dysfunctional way. She wasn't a get-along kind of feline, except when it came to Norma. Elaina hated to give up on the cat, yet Norma's offer to take her was a relief. "The two of you bonded right away. You're buddies. I'll poll the others. I'm sure they'll agree that Lula would be better off with you."

A smile took hold of Norma's face and didn't let go. "She's sort of a service animal for me. When she's near, I'm calm and that's really saying something. At work, I'm a hundred-miles-an-hour waitress who can handle ten tables at a time. Things change when I'm alone. I think about all the things that should've happened in my life but didn't and I turn into a hot mess. It would mean the world to me to be able to come home to that sweet cat."

Calling Lula a sweet cat was a huge stretch of anyone's imagination. "Could you give me a minute? I want to get Lula's take on things."

"Sure. Take your time."

In the living room, Elaina got down on all fours, and smashed her cheek against the carpet to peek under the loveseat.

Lula cowered away.

"Come here, Lula. We need to talk."

Obstinate as ever, Lula backed into the corner.

Elaina slid her fingers under the loveseat, trying to stroke Lula's toes.

Protective of her territory, the cat batted Elaina's hand.

Elaina took another stab at establishing a connection. "Listen, you stubborn ball of fur, I rescued you. I tried to reunite you with your owner. When my effort fell flat, I brought you home. You were shy, but you eventually made up with me. Now you run like I'm a stranger. Are you pissed that you have to share the attention with Stony...and now Bailey?"

"Your rump in the air – now that's a painting." Grace walked by and slapped Elaina on the tush.

"I'm trying to have a chat with Lula."

"Stop embarrassing yourself. It ain't gonna happen. Mornin', Norma. Ohhh pancakes!"

"Watch out for the bottle of syrup, it's tricky."

Tawny walked by and tried to shove her over.

"Lula, I'm giving you to the count of three to come to me. After that, I'm moving the loveseat."

"Booyah!"

Elaina removed her attention from the cat and put it on Grace, who was aiming her phone at her. "You did not take my picture."

"Mmm-hmm." Grace checked the photo. "I'm saving that for our Christmas card."

"Delete the photo right now or be prepared to have your phone dunked in the toilet." Elaina jumped up and took off after Grace. She snagged a fistful of her shirt and heard a loud rip. "My bad."

Steph met them at the base of the stairs. "I'm not even going to ask."

Grace egged Elaina on. "Caption: Does this picture

make my butt look big?"

With lightning speed, Elaina stole the phone and ran down the hall, into the laundry room.

At the click of the lock, Grace pounded on the door. "Do not destroy the picture. It's my property."

"My keister is copyrighted. You can't use it without my permission."

"Okay. I surrender to pancakes, not you."

The clip clop of shoes on the tiled floor alerted Elaina to Grace's retreat. She inched open the door. The hallway was clear.

"Don't mind Elaina. She's having a midlife meltdown. Today's her birthday." Grace propped against the counter and commenced drinking her coffee.

"I'm NOT having a midlife meltdown."

"How do you explain being on all fours, begging the cat to love you."

Elaina broke into a maniacal laugh. She held her belly and snorted several times.

"See what I mean? Meltdown."

Elaina whapped Grace on the arm and dropped the phone on her pancakes. "Keep the picture. Put it on our Christmas card. Put it on a billboard. I don't give a flying fig." She stuck her butt toward Grace. "Snap a few more. My backside is toned and shapely."

"Do you know what would make the picture even more hilarious?"

Elaina hooded her eyes in a fake glare. "Do tell."

"If you put on my catwoman mask."

"Catwoman mask?"

Steph shared with Norma the tale of giving Grady – Tawny's ex – a bit of payback for dumping Stony's things on Elaina's front yard. "We waited until dusk. Dressed all in black, we sneaked from tree to tree. Grace donned the mask. It was the funniest damn thing. We almost gave ourselves away by laughing. Like cat burglars, we padded around his property and smeared Crisco shortening on his mailbox, screen door handle, welcome mat, trashcan lid, and car antenna." At Norma's questioning grin, she mentioned Grady had an aversion to certain textures. "We wanted to karate chop his neck. At Elaina's insistence, we chose a non-physical approach."

"Is there anything you girls won't do?"

Tawny took the question. "I wouldn't rob a bank or deface a statue. Would I do the polar plunge in the Atlantic? I think not. Frostbite on the jubblies would not feel good. I'd never eat fish head soup."

"We get the idea. Would you give up our cat for a good cause?"

* * *

Steph stepped past Nicholas and looked around. "Where's all your stuff?"

"I brought the essentials."

Her forehead lined with confusion. "I thought this was to be your permanent residence."

Elaina tried not to listen in on their conversation, but she'd been in the process of cleaning the woodwork in the living room when he arrived. The whole place smelled like pine disinfectant.

"Steph, darlin', I'm not a one-night stand. I'm here for the long haul. To keep from cluttering the bed and breakfast, I stored most of my things in the shed behind the restaurant. You have almost everything I need, so I only brought the basics – my grooming kit and clothes, especially the suit I bought for my son's wedding."

"Their big day is fast approaching."

Nicholas blew out a breath. "I'm happy for Nick the second and Margaret, but I'm not looking forward to the wedding. My ex will be there with her new man. She's a pain in my neck and he's a douche."

"I'll be there to help you through it."

Nicholas pulled Steph into his chest. "I know you will be. I'm still bringing plenty of bail money in case things go south."

Steph ran her hands through his hair. "Your ex has no idea what she let go."

"Stephanie Mathews, I'm deeply in lust with you and my heart is overflowing with love."

Grace stuck her head out of the library nook, where she was straightening their assortment of books, magazines, and DVD's. "Get a room."

Laughter zipped all around.

Tawny ambled down the stairs and dropped into a recliner.

Grace left her post in the nook and sat in the recliner next to Tawny. "I have news to share." She channeled a smile to Elaina. "It's not about your birthday. I'll get to that in a little bit." Her backside hadn't even sunk into the cushion when she scooted out of the chair and traipsed to the window.

Tawny slapped a hand to her forehead. "Please don't tell me you're moving in with Philip."

"I'm not," Grace parted the curtains, "at least not yet, and not at his current place." She pointed to the old three-story Victorian house across the street that had a For Sale sign shoved down in the snow. "Philip absolutely loves that place. It needs a lot of work, but it has so much potential. He's going to call the realtor and arrange a showing." She rubbed her hands together. "My address might change by one number."

Elaina and Tawny exchanged open-mouth looks of surprise.

Tawny recovered from the shock first. "Shut the front door!"

Steph remarked that it was all ready closed.

Grace wasted no time informing Steph it was a figure of speech.

"I'm forty, not ninety. I'm well aware it's something people say to keep from flinging around the f-bomb."

Nicholas smirked. "I did not know that, Steph."

"Forty is the new thirty. Fifty is the new forty. You'd never know it by you dorks." Grace turned to Tawny. "IF we buy the place, it could be six months before the place is livable, so don't freak out."

"I'm not freaking out. I. Just. Don't. Want. You. To. Leave." Tawny bore down on Grace with a firm look and then she swung it to Nicholas. "Don't even think about taking Steph away from us."

"We have no immediate plans for her to leave the nest."

Elaina wrung out the cloth she'd been using to clean the woodwork and tried not to weigh in. Change was inevitable, but like Tawny, she wasn't ready for people to drop out of the picture.

"When and if I relocate my belongings to Philip's new place," Grace used her fingers to imitate walking, "use those legs and come on over."

Tawny chuffed out a sigh. "I need wine. Does anybody else need wine?"

* * *

Nicholas put them in a private party room in the back of the restaurant. "My son will take good care of us this evening and the celebration is on me." He handed out menus and gave each person a wine list.

Tawny spoke up. "You're part of the clan, thus not responsible for the tab. This is your livelihood, Nick."

Jess's dreamy gaze met Elaina's. "I'd like to foot the bill for your birthday, if you don't mind."

"You don't have to do that. Seriously, it's just another day."

"You'll only turn forty-four once. Annnnd, it's my way of saying thanks."

Everyone stopped what they were doing and gave Jess their consideration.

"Has she been sneaking out to the loft in the middle of the night?"

Before Elaina could react, Jess said, "Only in my dreams."

Something warm and wonderful exploded in Elaina. She wanted to take Jess by the shoulders and kiss him senseless.

He clutched her hand. "Because of Elaina, I've lost ten pounds and my A1C numbers are dropping."

"You romantic devil you," Grace spouted.

"Does that mean we can't have cake?" Tawny whined.

"You can have whatever you like. The only temptation for me is Elaina."

A blush started in Elaina's face and traveled all the way down to her toes.

Tawny never missed an opportunity to tease. "Better watch out. She's very sweet. One taste and you'll..."

Elaina chopped the air. "Stop right there, Tawn'."

Everyone at the crowded table laughed.

Nick-the-second came to Elaina and stooped to give her his undivided attention. "The birthday girl gets to go first. What can I get you?"

"The salmon lettuce wraps sound delicious."

Eyes the color of Nicholas-the-first's twinkled with satisfaction. "You'll love the spicy mayo. It's my own recipe."

"I can't wait to try it. Do the wraps come with onion?"

"Are green onions, okay?"

"Certainly." Elaina winked at Jess. "I'm getting extra onion, better kiss me now." Expecting him to laugh and dive into the cracker basket setting in front of him, she took a sharp breath when he took her face in his hands and brushed her lips with a soft kiss. The mere touch of their mouths rousted a more intense heat and sent it rushing through every vein and capillary in her body. In the cozy lighting of the restaurant, they stared at one another.

Grace played with Philip's ponytail. "Are you seeing this? He's looking at her like she's a hot fudge sundae."

"I'll have to speak with him about that. He's making the rest of us guys look bad."

Elaina snapped out of the Jess-fog when Steph and Nicholas began singing Happy Birthday. Their rendition of the age old song was as bad as a record player needle scratching across a vinyl album, but it made her smile.

They didn't sing the song just once, they kept it up. After the third time, Elaina wiggled a finger in her ear. "Okay, thank you. Now that you got that out of your system, let's move on. You're impeding Nick-the-second from taking food orders."

"I'll have the salmon wraps too." Under the table, Jess touched her knee with his. "Also with extra onion."

Steph and Nicholas decided to go with a salad they invented and would become part of their cookbook. It involved iceberg lettuce, baby spinach, kale, quinoa, avocado, bell peppers, jalapeno, cucumber, peas, green onions, a sprinkle of fresh parmesan on top, and garlic-parmesan dressing.

"Keep eating like a rabbit and you'll be able to hop around those 47,000 acres, Nick," Bart joked.

"Ha. Ha," Nicholas quipped with good-natured sarcasm.

Everyone else ordered surf and turf.

It took a good hour for the meal to be eaten and the table to be cleared.

Elaina stood. "Excuse me. It's time to powder my nose."

Tawny, Steph, and Grace echoed her announcement.

"Four women going to the ladies room at the same time. That can't be good." Philip leaned back in his chair and took a drink of beer.

"Afraid you'll be the topic of hushed conversation?"

"I'm afraid I'll have to start doing the hot fudge sundae thing."

Elaina laughed herself out of the room.

* * *

In the restroom, Tawny, Steph, and Grace formed a tight circle around Elaina. She straight-armed Grace who was closest to the stall. "When I said I had to powder my nose, it meant I had to pee. Do you mind stepping aside?"

"First things first." Grace raised and lowered her brows several times. "I have a present for you."

"We don't do birthday presents. Now move out of the way or I'm going to pee on your shoe."

"Better hurry, Grace. She must have to go really bad, her eyes are turning yellow." Tawny turned on the faucet.

The noise of running water brought things to the critical stage. Elaina squeezed her thighs together. "You wicked, wicked woman."

Tawny chortled.

Elaina shoved Grace out of the way, stepped into the stall, and locked the door. "Ahhhh, sweet relief."

They waited for her to wash her hands and then pounced again.

Grace opened her clutch purse and produced a small gift wrapped in tissue paper. She'd drawn a smiley face on the paper. "For you, boss lady."

Again Elaina reiterated that they didn't do presents.

"Stop whining and start opening."

Elaina ripped apart the delicate paper and moaned at the gift inside. "How thoughtful." She held up a packet with a ribbed condom inside and one that contained 'special' lube. "Thank you. I'm touched," she said with a boatload of snark.

Grace backhanded her on the arm. "I'm sure they won't be put to good use tonight. Extra onion? What were you thinking?"

Chapter Eleven

~ Bring on the pain! ~

Elaina met Jess coming out of the private room of the restaurant.

Jess took her hand. "Alyssa called. Her boyfriend ditched her for someone named Clarice. To make matters worse, she's struggling with a few classes – in part due to the girl she shares a dorm room with. The girl parties nonstop and 'Lyss has to go elsewhere to study. She's a mess and needs me." He moved his hands to her waist. "I hate to leave, especially on your birthday."

Elaina's heart sunk, but Jess had made it plain that he'd always be there for his daughter – and he should be. She stepped on her tiptoes and gave him a quick peck on the mouth. "There's nothing better for Alyssa right now than having you there. I'm sorry her world is in an uproar, but I'm glad you're going to help her through it."

"I'm not sure when I'll be back. This could take a while."

"No worries. Really. Family first."

"You're an amazing woman." He gave her a hasty kiss, and just like that, he was gone.

Tawny brought Elaina a glass of blackberry wine. "Where's he going in an all-fired hurry?"

"To visit his daughter in Virginia."

"You and I seem to have the worst luck when it comes to men and hot nights of romance."

"I'm not up for a hot night of romance anyway."

"Yes you are. You just haven't had one for a while."

"I'm not sure I've EVER had one." Elaina clasped Tawny's forearm. "Why are you having the worst luck? You said Bart's not the one, yet you're still together. Is the problem that he's unable to…you know."

"It's okay to say erectile dysfunction. Geez, Elaina. You don't have to ease your way around words. Just say them. Cuss once in a while too. That way I won't feel bad when I do. Drop the f-bomb right now. I want to hear it come out of your mouth."

"Not going to happen."

"Come on."

"No."

"Make me proud. Say it."

"F…" Elaina laughed. "No can do."

Tawny held up a finger. "One time and I'll leave you alone."

"You need serious help."

"No I don't. Neither does Bart. He's ready, willing, and able to do…you know."

* * *

"Pick up the pace, ladies. We have guests coming in less than an hour." Grace shouted out orders like she was made for the job. "Tawny get your bottom to the airport STAT. Steph, the kitchen looks like you detonated a flour bomb. Elaina," she hesitated.

"Don't stop now, you're on a roll."

Grace crossed her arms. "Elaina, you used the snow blower earlier. The way the wind's whipping around, the sidewalks and porches could use another go. You might also want to scatter some salt. We don't want anyone coming in for a crash landing."

Elaina traded looks of amusement with Tawny. They bestowed synchronized salutes on Grace. "I like when she takes charge."

"That's because you're weird." Tawny wrapped a scarf around her neck. "The van will be packed with people. I may have to make two trips."

"I could follow you in my Escalade."

"And go against Grace's orders? I think not."

"Change in plans. There's no way ten people can fit into the van comfortably with luggage. There might be skis to deal with as well. Elaina, follow Tawny. I'll tend to the sidewalks."

"Spoken like a true manager. We're on it."

Grace cocked a commanding eyebrow. "Rib me all you want. When guests are here, we have to give them our best."

"You're the one who always wants to be naughty, but okay, we'll be good."

Grace's sigh was filled with frustration – it might've

been fake, it might've been real. It was anybody's guess.

Tawny toned down her lighthearted unruliness. "All the clowning around will stop the second we greet the guests. Until then, have a few slugs of Fireball whisky to calm your nerves."

* * *

While they waited for the flight from Georgia to arrive, Tawny took a seat on a bench near luggage carousel number one in Baggage Claim. "Grace was tense today."

"It's probably the fear of menopause messing with her again. She'll be fine in a day or two."

"Can I say something without ticking you off?"

Elaina was mildly jarred by the implication of wrongdoing on her part. "Of course you can."

A trace of anger settled into Tawny's tone. "I'm not sure I'm going to word this right, so bear with me." She shifted on the bench and avoided Elaina's eyes. "When one of us has a problem or issue, you gloss over it and say 'everything's going to be fine.'"

"Would you rather I say 'it's going to suck?'"

"No."

"Then what?"

"I don't know. It's just that sometimes all that sugary optimism is hard to take."

Hurt infiltrated Elaina's happiness and tears gathered behind her eyes. There were so many things she could say right now – none of them with sugary optimism. "You want me to be negative?"

"You're missing my point."

The red light rotated on the carousel, followed by a throng of anxious passengers ready to grab their luggage.

Tawny moved near the entrance and held up the Four Sassy Chicks sign.

Elaina looked around, at nothing in particular; trying to handle the prick meted out by the person who usually made her laugh. Emotion came at her like flood waters, ready to destroy her if she didn't act fast. She straightened from a slouch, took a stout breath, and put a mental bandage over her wounded feelings.

"Sassy chicks," a male voice hollered.

Tawny smiled. Elaina did the same.

"I'm Jake and this is Marcy. It's nice to meet y'all."

The rest of the entourage introduced themselves.

"I'm Elaina." She bypassed introducing Tawny.

The tight way Tawny said her own name was an indication she wasn't pleased to be slighted.

How's that for unsweetened cheerfulness?

They helped load luggage onto three carts. Fortunately there were no skis to contend with.

One of the men complained that the girls brought a ridiculous amount of clothes.

Elaina couldn't remember his name. Hank stuck in her head, but she didn't want to be wrong, so she just bared her teeth in a grin and said, "Girls need stuff."

A buxom blonde put her hand up for a high-five.

And the mayhem was officially underway. The guys and three-fourths of the luggage were loaded into the van with Tawny. The girls chose to ride with Elaina.

Marcy held up her phone. "Jake says we have to make a pit stop for beer and wine."

"At a bar?"

"A grocery, supermarket, or gas station would work. We want to buy it by case." Another alert ping indicated a second message. "The guys are starving. Could you take us to the nearest pizza joint that makes lobster pizza and a side of deep fried oysters?"

The redhead sitting in the front passenger seat mentioned that oysters were an aphrodisiac. Her casual statement opened the door to a semi-naughty discussion about the types of food, drink, and drugs known to stimulate sexual desire.

Elaina laughed to herself, remembering a similar conversation with Tawny, Steph, and Grace not so long ago.

Marcy informed Elaina that Madison needed something from a drugstore. Madison wouldn't say what it was, but given the present conversation Elaina had an inkling it had to do with personal protection. Maybe she should refer her to Grace.

"After we get the pizza would be fine," Jeannette said.

Elaina came close to informing her passengers that she wasn't taxi service, just transportation to and from the airport. Since she'd already pissed off Tawny, she didn't want a slew of others to be upset with her too. "Tomorrow I'd be happy to take you to a car rental place. They have vans that will seat ten."

"Or y'all could lend us your van," came a voice from the backseat.

"Our insurance carrier would throw a fit. They made it abundantly clear who could and could not drive the vehicle.

"Well phooey."

Snowflakes began to cascade down from the clouds and land on the windshield.

"We live on the Georgia-Florida border and seldom see snow. This will be a real treat."

"We're originally from Ohio and occasionally got snow. This is our first winter in Maine and we're still trying to wrap our heads around the constant precip."

"Have you skied? Or gone snowboarding?"

"We haven't."

"Maybe you could take us," the same voice said from the backseat.

Elaina looked in the rearview mirror and identified the person speaking as the blonde she'd given a high-five to at the jetport. "Sorry. No can do." Some whispering commenced directly afterward.

If the ride from the airport to the bed and breakfast was a sign of how things would go during their visit, it would be a long week and there was potential for another one-star review.

Elaina said the f-bomb under her breath. Too bad Tawny wasn't there to hear it.

* * *

"It took you long enough."

"Not now, Steph."

"Did I hit a nerve?"

"No. You're *fine*. Everything's going to be *fine*." Elaina deliberately put inflection on the word fine to get under Tawny's skin.

"I'll give our guests the grand tour. You can take care of their luggage." Tawny didn't wait for a reaction."

"What's with her?"

"I wish I knew. Where's Grace?"

Steph put her hands on each side of her head. "She fell while trying to use the snow blower. That thing has more power than she could handle."

They'd all experienced close calls when it came to falling. Elaina had taken a spill, luckily without breaking anything. "Is she all right?"

"She says her lower back hurts."

Elaina went flying past Tawny and the guests. She climbed the steps two at a time until she reached the third floor. "Grace?"

Grace's facial expression said she was in a lot pain. A series of whimpers confirmed it.

"I should've warned you about the snow blower. It tries to wrestle me every time I use it." Elaina sat on the edge of the bed. "We should take you to the ER to get you checked out. You could've cracked a vertebra or damaged a disc."

"I'm not going to the ER."

"Do I have to go full commandant on you?"

"You can beg until you're blue in the face. I'm not going to the hospital."

Elaina scratched her forehead. "I'm going to get

Tawny. She'll know what to do."

"Don't you dare! She'll call the squad and they'll strap me to a gurney. And I... Ugh! Just don't."

Tawny peeked around the door. "Steph tells me you wiped out."

"Kill me now," Grace muttered between clenched teeth.

"Tell me where it hurts."

"At the very base of my back, where my butt begins."

Tawny twisted her mouth in deliberation. "We're taking you to the hospital."

"No. You. Are. Not. It's my decision. I'm not going."

Tawny let out a string of unique groaning noises. "This couldn't have happened at a worse time. There are ten people downstairs counting on us to make their stay special."

"I didn't plan on getting hurt. One minute I was upright, the next I was flat on the concrete." Grace winced at a stabbing pain.

"You're putting me in a difficult position, Grace. I'm a nurse. I know what needs to take place."

"I knew you'd play the nurse card."

"Okay, be obstinate. You're the one who will suffer for it. Since you won't go to the hospital, you're getting ibuprofen and an ice pack."

"Won't heat work better?"

"Grace, you have to at least let me play nurse or I'm going to scream. For the first twenty-four to seventy-two hours, it's cold therapy to reduce selling. You can ice your back for twenty minutes at a time, no more than that. After we exhaust the cold, we go to heat, which will stimulate healing."

"Could you write that down? My mind's a little fuzzy."

"Did you hit your head as well?"

"No. All your chatter is putting me to sleep."

"I give up. I freaking give up." Tawny stormed out of the room.

"You'd think she was the one in pain."

Elaina shrugged. "I've got nothing."

* * *

"How are you?"

"Elaina?" Philip sounded surprised. Why wouldn't he be?

She'd made an executive decision to get him involved. Grace wouldn't be happy, but hey, sometimes you had to do things for the greater good. "Yes, it's me. I have a special request."

"You want to pose nude for me."

"Is that all you think about?"

"Not really, but it gets your goat every time. What's up, doll?"

"How do I say this without throwing you into a state of alarm?" She didn't give him room to think. "Your honey became one with the sidewalk."

The humor in Philip's voice vanished. "How bad is it?"

"Yet to be determined. Your bullhead of a girlfriend refuses to seek medical care."

"I'll be right there."

In ten minutes flat, he rang the door bell.

"How did you get here so fast? You live across town."

"It's a city, not a town."

"Semantics. How did you get from there to here without spinning out on the icy roads? Or without getting a speeding ticket?"

"I was on my way over to see Grace. You know how I like to show up without warning."

"Translation: we have ten guests and you wanted to check them out."

Philip pointed to Elaina. "Bingo." He scanned the living room. "Where's the patient?"

"Third floor, last door on the right."

"You could've said her bedroom."

"I also could've said city instead of town."

"You definitely have the sassy part of your business down pat." He looked toward the staircase. "Ready or not, stubborn wench, here I come."

"Good luck."

"I don't need luck, I have muscles."

Steph left the family room where the party of ten were watching Jeopardy. They'd formed teams to answer the questions along with the TV contestants – guys against the girls. Every time a guy got a wrong answer, he had to take a drink of beer. Every time a girl flubbed the answer, she had to have a gulp of wine. It was win-win, no matter what. "Philip."

"Stephanie."

Steph gave Elaina a questioning look.

"I called him."

"Ohh that's not good. Grace will not be happy."

"I happened to be in the neighborhood. Besides, I would've eventually found out that she's injured."

"You don't have to convince me. Grace is the one you'll have to persuade."

"I'll take the heat." Elaina led the way upstairs. She knocked on Grace's door. "You have company."

"It better not be an EMT."

Elaina stepped out of the way to grant Philip entry. "She's all yours, muscle-man."

"Music to my ears." He flicked the lamp on. "Hey, blue eyes."

Grace didn't yell. Instead, her voice was soft and quivery when she said Philip's name.

Elaina got to the kitchen in time to see Nick come in the back door. He swept Steph in his arms and nuzzled her neck. She started to back out to give them some catch-up time, but Tawny brushed past her and propped against the counter to look out the window. She was oblivious to the sweet romance going on near the wine rack. Fisting her hands, she hit the edge of the sink.

Nick let go of Steph.

Steph didn't look pleased. "Geez, Tawn'. Give us a break with the bad mood all ready."

That was Nick's cue to head upstairs. "See you in a bit, Steph?"

"You know it." She blew him a kiss.

Tawny sifted air through her teeth, waiting for Nick to ascend the stairs. She left her perch by the sink and made sure the coast was clear before engaging in a low-volume rant. "We have so much to learn when it comes to operating a bed and breakfast. How do we establish and convey ground rules without coming off as a bunch of cranky old women?"

Steph pointed out that the guests currently staying were older than them, which earned her a scowl.

Elaina threw herself on Tawny's fire. "There's a learning curve to any new venture. We knew the basics going in and we've done all right. The guests we've had so far have been easy, unless you count Persimmon Daniels. She came on strong a few times."

"Who could forget Persimmon? Your former classmate had changed her name to PerMission. She was bossy, peculiar, and beautiful in a punk-girl kind of way."

"She definitely wanted the upper-hand, Steph."

"You didn't back down."

"I'm not a pushover. I may come across that way sometimes, but I'm not." Elaina didn't meet Tawny's eyes.

"I don't know how you won her over, but you did, and for a while it looked like she would stay on as a member of the wine club."

Tawny had sighed between each of their comments. A hoot and holler from the family room sent her over the edge. "Ten people in one party are too much! If we had other guests, things would get tricky."

"But we don't have other guests." Steph touched Tawny's arm.

Tawny flinched away.

Steph tried again, this time without making physical

contact. "I don't know what's going on inside that noggin, but for our guests' sake you have to calm down. Let's all take a deep breath and we'll get through the week with our sanity intact."

To their surprise, Tawny actually took a deep breath.

Steph continued, "When they leave, we'll hash out what went right and what we need to fix."

At someone's boisterous, 'Yeah, baby, that's what I'm talking about,' Tawny tensed up again. "They're grinding my last nerve."

"Wanna practice doing facials on each other?"

"Get real. We're not offering facials and mani-pedis. It was a stupid idea." Tawny left the kitchen in a huff.

"Bart must've done something to get in her craw and she's taking it out on us."

"That's probably it." Yeah, no, it wasn't. Elaina wouldn't clue Steph into the things Tawny had said earlier. Those words still stung.

Chapter Twelve

~ Much to discover! ~

It was well after midnight before the five couples retreated to their rooms.

Elaina gathered beer cans for recycling, while Steph loaded wine glasses and snack plates in the dishwasher. Tawny had given up on the chaos and went to bed an hour earlier.

Steph grabbed a bottle of all-purpose disinfectant cleaner and a handful of cloths from the closet just off the kitchen.

"Steph, I'll get it. Nick is waiting upstairs for you."

"I can't abandon you."

Steph meant she couldn't let her finish tidying the place up, but her comment projected straight to Elaina's heart and the ruckus she'd had with Tawny that she was trying so hard not to think about, barreled to the surface. Her eyes watered right away and she covered the reaction with a fake sneeze. "You're not welching on clean-up duty. You've busted your butt all day. Go see Nick before his lights go out."

"He's probably snoring as we speak."

"Go spoon with him anyway. I've got this."

"Thanks, Elaina." Steph made it to the doorway. "I hope Grace is okay."

"Chances are she just bruised her back. We'll know more in the morning."

"Is Tawny going to be okay too? One day she's the Tawny we know and love; the next, she's a bitchy basket case."

"I don't know what to make of it or how to fix it. One thing's for sure, she's not herself."

"Do you think she needs professional help? Or medication?"

Elaina's eyes watered again. "Time will tell."

"I'll pray about it."

"Me too."

"See you bright and early."

In a matter of minutes, Elaina was surrounded by silence. She scrubbed the kitchen until every inch of the counter, every cabinet handle, everything anyone could've touched – sparkled. The tiled floor of the kitchen and dining areas had the appearance a stampede of buffalo had charged through. Elaina swept and mopped until all traces of buffalo were gone. Next, she tackled the dining area and the family room. They weren't in too bad of shape considering the guys had spent the bulk of the day there. She cleaned surfaces, picked up an ace of spades and a ten of clubs that had hidden themselves under the table, and ran the cordless vacuum.

By two o'clock, the place was restored to normal and it should've smelled great, but essence of sauerkraut seeped into the air. Steph had relocated the ceramic crock to the breezeway, but hints of pungent stench came through the duct work.

Elaina wandered back to the kitchen and took one last look around. Her eyes went to the corner where she'd found Tawny's diamond and the spigot of her tightly held emotions turned on.

* * *

Philip and Nick sat at the long dining table with the guests. They laughed and carried on with the male half of the party of ten. Red Sox baseball spring training that would soon take place became a lively discussion. Disagreements about the team's best players drove the women away from table.

Marcy joined Elaina, Tawny, and Steph in the kitchen. "There's too much testosterone flinging around in there."

Steph allied herself with Marcy. "I hear ya, sista. All that sports talk can erode a girl's ear canal."

"Good way to put it." Marcy stole a sausage link from the skillet. "Your bed and breakfast is even better than I imagined and y'all have made us feel at home."

Elaina and Steph said, "Thank you." Tawny seemed to be in her own little world. She was twitchy this morning and flitted around like a mosquito.

"The girls and I want to shop today. As ridiculous as it sounds, we're eager to buy moose-wear – tee's sunglasses, towels, anything and everything moose. The guys plan to hang around here and play cards again, if y'all don't mind."

Steph shook her head. "We don't mind. They'll have to contend with the occasional sound of a vacuum cleaner. We try to stay ahead of the dog hair."

"Oh we know about dog hair. Jake and I have two Corgis. They're double coated and shed year round. If we miss a day or two of vacuuming, there's enough hair lying around to make a third dog." Marcy grinned. "Your big dog keeps sniffing me. I think he smells Twyla and Benji."

"He likes to put his nose where it doesn't belong." Elaina nudged Tawny with her elbow. "Right, Tawn'?"

Tawny still hadn't tuned into the conversation. "What?"

"I said Stony discovers all there is to know about a person by putting his nose in our special place."

"Uh, yeah. He does. I've tried to break him of the habit."

Marcy laughed. "My dogs would do it too, but their legs are too short. Your Pomsky's feet are the same."

The blonde with hair that fell to her waist, flounced into the kitchen. "Can I get another cup of that delicious coffee?"

"You sure can." All the women's names started with M. For the life of Elaina, she couldn't remember the blonde's. She ran down the list in her head: Marcy, Morene, Morgan, Michelle, and Madison, trying to decide which one fit. "Morgan."

"No. I'm Morene."

"Sorry."

"It's okay." Morene sidled next to Marcy. "Did you ask her?"

Marcy's expression went from bubbly to getting-caught-with-her-hand-in-the-cookie-jar. "Not yet," she said out of the side of her mouth.

Marcy had been sent to butter them up.

Elaina encouraged Marcy to roll out the question, even though she had an inkling what it would be. "Go ahead and ask."

"You're going to say no."

How could she say no after miscalling Morene, Morgan? "The answer's yes. I'll take you to buy moose-wear." She anticipated some throat clearing from Steph and Tawny. They didn't fail her. Steph was the first to dislodge a fake furball from her throat. Tawny seconded the warning with a strident cough. "Ladies, this is a one-time deal. The only reason I'm taking you to the mall is because we could use some moose-wear around here too. Capish?"

Marcy slanted Morene a sly grin. "Capish."

"Is it safe to come in?" Philip leaned so they could see him.

"Why wouldn't it be?" Steph asked innocently.

"When women get together, they talk about stuff men don't want to hear."

Marcy zinged Philip. "You mean like male pattern baldness and toenail fungus?"

Philip's mouth dropped open.

Elaina knuckled-bumped Marcy. "You just earned a second girls-only outing." She was afraid to look at Steph and Tawny.

Stony whimpered from the other side of the kitchen gate. He didn't want to be left out of the fun.

"You don't want in here, boy. These women will sass you, big time."

Preparing breakfast for so many people had taken effort from all three women, leaving little time for chit chat. Now that everyone was fed, it gave them time to breathe and socialize, and time to inquire about Grace Vivian. "How's the blue-eyed sasser doing this morning?"

"Mulish as ever. Her back isn't swollen or black and blue. She says it only hurts a little." Philip began filling a plate. "Does she like eggs?"

Steph was in her element. "Pile them on." She handed him the jar of dill spice. "Grace loves dill on her eggs."

"Seriously?"

"Would I lie?"

Marcy whispered to Philip, but she'd said it loud enough for everyone to hear, "The right answer is no."

Elaina tilted her head toward Marcy. "Now she's working you, instead of me. She's vying for a third girls-only outing, with you as their driver."

They all laughed.

Philip put two tomato slices on the plate. "What else does she like?"

"Salsa dancing."

He snorted a laugh. "Women! Just when you think you're one step ahead of them, you discover you're not."

* * *

"You've got to see this shopping plaza. There are over a hundred stores and I swear the M-ladies have visited each one twice. I finally turned them loose, bought a white chocolate mocha espresso, and took a seat on a bench. They've been instructed to meet me here in an hour," Elaina checked her watch, "which will be up in ten minutes."

"The guys don't seem to notice the women are gone. They're still playing cards, drinking beer, and calling each other colorful names. Grace made it out of bed. She's walking slow and slightly hunched over. Tawny has resting-bitch-face, but she's washing the mound of bed linens and towels like a laundry ninja. Stony and Bailey have been running around like crazy dogs. Funniest thing yet: when Stony has enough of Bailey jumping at him or nipping at his ankles, he lays on her to make her stop."

"That's a whole lot of mayhem under one roof."

"Did you buy me a moose tee?"

"Maybe." Elaina had made some special purchases. They were perfect for their four-member wine club. Because of the tense state of affairs with Tawny, she possibly would hold onto the gifts for a while.

"What is it?"

"You'll have to wait and see. I might keep it until Christmas."

"That's just plain mean."

Elaina laughed, for more reasons than Steph trying to extract the FYI on the gift. Coming at her were the five M's wearing moose hats. "You are not going to believe this. Hold on, Steph. I'm going to send you a picture. Do not show it to the guys. Let the girls surprise them."

A few seconds later, Steph roared with laughter. "The hats have antlers!"

"I have to go. We'll see you soon, hopefully."

Elaina cocked her head one way and then the other. "Ladies, you look fabulous."

"We definitely do." Madison struck a sexy pose and snapped a selfie. "Now a group picture."

The women gathered close together and Elaina took turns using their phones to capture the moment. She was sure by the time they got back to Four Sassy Chicks the pictures will have circled the world three times via Facebook, Twitter, and Instagram.

Michelle took a candy box out of one of her many bags. "Would you care for a dark-chocolate salted caramel? Or a hand-dipped truffle?"

Elaina sampled a caramel. "Oooo! Heaven in a little tiny square."

The other ladies raided the box until it was empty.

Michelle's bottom lip plumped in a pout. "They're gone." She tossed the empty box in the trash. "I have to go back for another one."

Marcy nixed that idea right out of the gate. "It's almost dinner time, 'Chelle. Tonight we're going to eat all the succulent lobster in Maine."

Morene adjusted the hat so it wouldn't encumber her

long hair. "I hope the guys have rented a van or Elaina will have to cart us to dinner."

"Morene, you're a hoot." Elaina jerked both thumbs at herself. "This taxi driver is off the clock the minute she pulls into the garage."

"Can we bribe you with a moose t-shirt?"

"You cannot."

"Would a set of moose salt and pepper shakers do the trick?"

"A five foot moose made of dark-chocolate salted caramel wouldn't do the trick."

"Phooey."

Elaina snickered at Morene's use of the word phooey again. "Grab your packages, ladies. We are headed home." She lagged in the rear and sent Steph another text. *If the guys haven't rented a van, they need to do so right away.*

Are the M girls trying to hornswaggle you into being their ride for this evening too?

Yes they are.

Pushover.

Yes I am. She'd told Jess she wasn't one. She'd told Tawny the same thing. Elaina shook her head at the inconsistency in her character – she let people push their way in and push her buttons while they were there. When the stakes were higher, however, no pushing was allowed.

* * *

Nicholas offered free appetizers if the group chose his dining establishment for dinner.

Marcy-the-schmoozer was at it again. "We'd love to, but we're currently lacking wheels."

The schmoozing swung from Marcy to Nicholas. "Steph, any chance you could deliver these fine people to our restaurant?"

"Our restaurant?"

"Of course, sweetheart."

Elaina was a hair away from rolling her eyes. Nicholas trumped Marcy when it came to butt kissing.

"Sure, babe, I'd be happy to." Under her breath, Steph informed Elaina that she was a pushover too.

A laughed leaped between them.

Grace hobbled from the bathroom and headed for the stairs. "As soon as Philip closes his gallery for the day, he's coming back to take care of me."

"Can I get you anything, Grace?"

"Yes, a gas mask."

Marcy's hubby, Jake spoke up. "I blamed the deadly fumes on Smitty. He denied passing gas. Usually, he's proud to take credit for stinking up the air."

Tawny walked through with an armload of towels. "Steph, either move the sauerkraut to the back of the lot or I'll haul it to the curb for the garbage men to dispose of it."

Smitty ran a tongue over his lips. "Do not haul it away. I love sauerkraut."

"That explains a lot," Jake taunted.

Smitty pushed Jake in fun. Jake pushed back, sending Smitty into a lamp table. Michelle's husband Craig got in on the action. Stony let out a yowl and Bailey barked.

Marcy grabbed a handful of Jake's coat. "You break a lamp, you buy a lamp." She gave him a high-eyebrow.

"Got it. Behave, guys." Jake pointed to the door. "We have crustaceans to consume."

And they were off.

Grace hobbled up the stairs.

Tawny distributed towels to bathrooms on the second floor.

Elaina grabbed a bottle of dry red from the wine rack and removed the cork. She listened for Tawny to mosey down the stairs and go into her bedroom. After pulling in a deep breath for courage, she knocked on Tawny's door. There was a long moment of nothingness. She knocked again. "Tawn', can I come in?"

The oak door muffled most of Tawny's reply, "If you feel you must."

Elaina made the Sign of the Cross and pleaded silently for strength. She entered and closed the door behind her, in case Tawny chose to bolt again. No way would Elaina chase her down after dark. With the snow melting during the day and refreezing at night, either one of them could end up in the same shape as Grace.

Tawny lay on her bed, staring at the TV even though it wasn't turned on.

Setting the bottle of wine and glasses on the dresser, Elaina took a seat beside Tawny on the bed. "We need to have a serious talk."

A grunt slid between Tawny's lips.

Swallowing her apprehension, Elaina began. "I don't understand your sudden animosity toward me, Tawn'.

Maybe it's not sudden. Maybe I'm just now picking up on it. I don't know. Maybe you've felt this way for a while and I was too caught up in trying to make things work that I didn't see the change. Does you giving me the cold shoulder stem from the winter blues or is it something more?"

"Stop! Just stop!"

Elaina recoiled.

"You didn't do anything wrong, okay?" Tawny's voice equaled a shout. "This is about me."

Trying not to light another stick of dynamite, Elaina softly asked, "Are you unhappy here?"

Tawny's chin dropped to her chest. "I'm unhappy, yes. It only has a little to do with being in Maine."

A noiseless sigh worked itself up and out of Elaina. She didn't know whether to risk another question. A few excruciating seconds ticked by without Tawny saying more.

"Please talk to me. I'm begging you. This thick wall of tension you've erected to keep me out isn't healthy for us."

Tawny contorted her body to look directly at Elaina. "You had a birthday party. I had a pity party."

Elaina went to speak, but Tawny shook her head. "Life throws handfuls of mud at you, yet you're able to walk away without any grime sticking. You have a love-hate relationship with your ex. Arden in his own bizarre way loves you. He couldn't live with you because barracudas make terrible bed partners. He still gives you an occasional headache, even though he respects and admires you. He'd never admit to any of it, but all of it is true. My ex no longer acknowledges I exist and my sons are following his lead. Most days my dog would rather hang out with you than me. Lula even liked you best, until Norma took over. And Bailey... I don't even have to go there. You know she thinks you're her mama." Tawny took a short breath and kept talking. "You have Jess wrapped around your pinkie. If you told him to stand on one foot and sing *When a Man Loves a Woman* he would."

"You're..." That's the only word Elaina got out before Tawny put a finger across her lips.

"Shh. Let me finish."

Elaina complied with the request.

"To top it all off, you're rich, beautiful, and have the same figure as you did when you were sixteen."

"Yeah, but you have boobs."

Tawny broke into an unexpected laugh.

Elaina hoped the off-the-wall, nonsensical comment was a catalyst to fixing whatever the hell was broken.

Tawny's mirth vanished as quickly as it had come. "If you tell me I'm wrong about any of it, you'd be lying."

Elaina frowned hard and decided not to let Tawny silence her. "Listen up, Tawn'." She flexed her hands several times. "You hurt me for no good reason. I totally get how you'd think everything is coming up roses for me, but deep in your heart you know your jaded perception isn't accurate. I don't know why you're keying on me and comparing your life to mine, but fine, I have broad shoulders. I'd rather you take pot shots at me, rather than at Steph and Grace. Whether you like it or not, I'm going to respond to each and every thing you said. Number one: I don't have the world by the tail. Not even close. Number two: You were blessed with two incredible boys. They ignore you because you let them. Number three: Grady might not acknowledge your existence, but he can't forget you're the woman he married and had kids with. On the flip side, when was the last time you acknowledged him or checked on him? Number four: Lula tolerated me because I bugged her endlessly with baby talk. She's found joy with Norma. I don't resent her for not loving me like I thought she should. Number five: Stony would die without you. If you think otherwise, then you're a damn fool. He cares about us, but the bulk of his affection is for you. Number six: Bailey? Yes, I could be her favorite. I won't apologize. Number seven…"

"Getting long-winded here."

"Deal with it. Where was I?"

"Number seven," Tawny quipped with a small amount of sarcasm.

"Thank you. Number seven: Jess isn't wrapped around my pinkie or any of my other fingers. If that was the case, I would've heard from him every day. He sent a text when he arrived in Virginia. I haven't heard from him since. Number eight…" Tawny's drawn out sigh didn't obstruct her from sharing her thoughts. "Number eight," she repeated, "I am not rich. I have a financial cushion. Again, no apology will be forthcoming. The money I have came via a divorce settlement. Who in their right mind can be happy about that? Number nine: Thanks for the compliment about my looks. I'm not beautiful, but I'm glad you think so. Regarding my figure, I'd rather have your torpedo boobs than my flat chest. You'll argue that your boobs are too much to deal with, but those of us that got slighted in the chest area will continue to tell you how lucky you are. I'm proud that my arms and legs have definition, but it took work to get them that way. Did I miss anything?" Tears pooled in her eyes while she waited for Tawny to either accept or heatedly criticize all nine points.

"No. You didn't miss a thing, but I did. I missed my best friend. I'm sorry, Elaina, so sorry." Tears also collected in Tawny's eyes. "You're the best thing that's happened to me in a long time and I've been trying to messed things up."

A little bit of Elaina's broken heart glued itself back together. "I missed you too." They were a long way from rectifying the issues, but she was ready to get back on level ground. "You'll hate when I say this, I'm going to say it anyway – Everything is going to be fine. We're fine. But we can't brush this episode of depression or whatever it might be, under the rug. I love ya, Tawn'. If you seriously have S.A.D., you need to talk to a professional or get a low dose medication to get you over the hump."

"As a nurse, I've been wracking my brain, trying to figure out what's wrong. I truly don't think I have S.A.D. I think it's my insecurities and my failures rearing their ugly heads. I won't pin the blame on my parents or on Grady, although they contributed to the problem. They expected perfection and I tried to be that person, I really did. Because I couldn't hold up my end, I let myself down and my sons. I know you'll argue that I didn't, in my mind I did."

Elaina gathered Tawny in her arms and kissed her head. "You put so much pressure on yourself. It's probably a parental side effect, and yes, Grady played a role in your lack of confidence, but you're so much more than you give yourself credit for. You're an awesome nurse and friend, and one hell of a bed and breakfast owner. Can I tell you a secret?"

"Of course."

"I'm going through some of the same uncertainties. That whole pregnancy thing with Arden and Rachel has just about done me in. I keep asking myself what I could've done differently. I wanted kids, Tawn'. I wanted a son or daughter or a dozen of each so badly. Arden all but shouted from the rafters that kids were pests and if I got pregnant on purpose he'd divorce me right away. I consider that two missed opportunities."

"Arden knows he screwed up. I'm sure if he could turn back time, he would treat you better and give you a slew of confident kids."

"I just pictured a bunch of little Arden's bossing me around." Elaina smiled, but followed up with a hard swallow. "Tawny, we have to rein in on all the commotion going on in our heads."

"It isn't the first time I've gone haywire and I'm sure it won't be the last. Starting over isn't easy. Not only does a person have to figure out where to go, what to do, how to stretch their finances so they don't lose everything, but also how to handle the emotional sneak attacks that come when we least expect them."

"You've nailed the reality of it. Back to square one is no fun. You know those handfuls of mud that get thrown at me?"

Tawny winced. "Sorry for wording it that way."

"No, no, that's precisely what happens. Some of the grime does stick." Elaina shoulder-bumped Tawny. "I hear you're a laundry ninja and can get out the worst stains."

"You mean I actually help you sometimes?"

"You do. You make me laugh a lot."

"I make you crazy too."

"There's more laughter than craziness."

"I truly don't know what I would do without you. Thank you for seeing me through this latest crisis. I want to help you through yours."

"You already have. As long as we have each other… and some wine…we'll get through those sneak attacks." Elaina eased off the bed and motioned for Tawny to do the same. "Let's take our bottle of wine upstairs. I'm sure Grace could use some company and a glass of vino medicine for her back."

Chapter Thirteen

~ Semi-normal is as good as it gets! ~

The rest of the week flew by with them waiting hand and foot on the party of ten. And yes, Marcy and the other M-girls made every excuse under the sun why they didn't have a rental vehicle. Elaina, Tawny, and Steph took turns hauling their butts here and there. Elaina grumbled, but truthfully, the M's were entertaining and the gloom of winter didn't seem intolerable. The refrigerator was stuffed with leftovers from the many seafood restaurants they dined at.

Marcy rolled her overstuffed piece of luggage to the back of the van. "Either my jeans shrunk or all that lobster dipped in butter has made my butt go up a pant size. My suitcase is overweight too."

"Tell me about it," Morene whined. "I had to lie on the bed and have Smitty pull the zipper up on my jeans. I'm afraid if I bend over my pants will split and everyone will know I'm wearing black lace underwear."

Smitty shook his head. "She loves telling people what

kind of underwear she has on."

"I do not."

"Do too."

"Do not."

The playful argument continued long after they were trapped in their seatbelts.

The other M-girls and their husbands held other conversations, leaving Elaina to her thoughts. She turned on the radio to drown out the background noise. Low and behold, A LITTLE BIT MORE by Dr. Hook was playing. She smiled, reliving the sweet memory of her time with Jess on the airplane. She wouldn't mind making a lot more memories with him; a few more intimate ones would be nice. First, he had to get back from Virginia. Elaina tried not to focus on the fact he'd only sent the one text since he'd left, but it bounced around in her head like an out of control ping pong ball.

Marcy broke into her thoughts. "I'm going to miss all this snow."

Morgan reminded her that they didn't make time to play in it.

"You're right. Stop the van! Stop the van!" Marcy said excitedly.

Elaina looked in the rearview mirror. "So you can play?"

"Just for a little bit."

The men groaned.

Against her better judgment, Elaina turned onto a side street so they could do whatever with snow.

Marcy, Morene, Morgan, Michelle, and Madison

jumped in a drift. Their husbands stood on the sidewalk shaking their heads.

"On our next vacation, it's men only." Smitty received a glare from Morene.

Madison's husband had been the quiet one of the group, until now. "Damned straight we're leaving the women folk at home. Look at them. You'd think they would've seized the opportunity to play in the snow long before now. But no, they waited until we're headed to the airport. Take off that stupid moose hat, Maddie."

"Make me, Theo."

He jammed his hands on his hips. "Don't think I won't."

Madison wrinkled her nose with amusement. "I'm not afraid of you."

"You should be."

"Show her who's boss, Theo." Jake received a poke in the ribs from Marcy.

Theo took Jake's advice and went after Madison. He grabbed her by the waist and mischievously tossed her butt-first into a mound of snow.

"Ohhhh, you're doing down, husband. Ladies, some assistance please."

Laughter rent the chilly air as Theo fought five women. With little difficulty, they turned him into a snowman.

The women hit their hands together to remove snow from their gloves. "Take that, Theodore."

In allegiance to their buddy, the men staged a retaliatory strike. Every M was the recipient of a snowball down the back of her coat or under her shirt.

Elaina had to intervene. "Your plane is due to take off in an hour and twenty minutes."

"Yes, Mom," Marcy teased.

Morene made Elaina's day, "Thank you for letting us act the fool, right now and during our entire stay. You've been incredible. We can be a lot to handle, but we're great friends who enjoy life."

"It's been a pleasure having you stay at our bed and breakfast, but more importantly, it's been a pleasure getting to know you." Elaina smiled. They obviously attracted the crazies, then again, they were just as wacky.

* * *

"Listen to how quiet it is," Grace said from the recliner. "I don't like it one bit."

Stony raised his head from where he was parked at Tawny's feet. He blinked at Grace as if saying, "Don't look at me. I can't make any noise because Bailey has worn me out."

Bailey was curled up next to Elaina. The little fur ball had jumped until she was placed in her lap, then went to sleep right away.

"Try this! Try this!" Steph ran into the living room with a dish and three forks.

"So much for quiet," Tawny said with a grin.

"What's this?"

"It's sauerkraut with a kick."

"More sauerkraut? Ugh!"

"Stop whining, Grace. This isn't the kraut from the

crock. I threw this together in a Mason jar a week ago. It's the bomb! Sadly, it's not an original recipe. It has cabbage, jalapeno, cilantro, garlic, onion, and sea salt. I wish I would've thought of it first. Here, have a bite." She shoved the dish at Grace and handed her a fork.

"All that cabbage has made you hyper. Are you about to blow from the gas?"

"Ha. Ha. One taste and you'll be thanking me instead of poking fun at me."

Grace sampled the kraut and her eyes rounded with surprise. "This is good stuff."

"What have I been trying to tell you? The big crock of sauerkraut is great too. I tried some earlier. It's packed with flavor."

Grace passed the dish around for the others to have a taste.

"My taste buds are doing the mamba right now, Steph. Seriously, this is delish'."

The change in Tawny's demeanor made Elaina smile. Together they'd worked through the kinks of their shortcomings and insecurities. For now, there was peace at the Four Sassy Chicks Bed and Breakfast.

* * *

Elaina woke with a weird feeling. At four-thirty in the afternoon it still hadn't gone away. She walked by the living room window in time to see a taxi cab pull up out front. The driver popped open the trunk and ran around to retrieve the passenger's luggage.

The man climbed out of the cab with his phone glued to his ear.

She leaned closer to the window to get a better look. Either her eyes were deceiving her or Jess had come home.

Jess looked over his shoulder, as if he knew he was being watched. Tucking his phone in his coat pocket, he paid the cabbie and trekked toward the back of the bed and breakfast.

Elaina ran out to the deck. "Jess, you're back!"

He smiled and abandoned his suitcase on the sidewalk. "Hey, pretty lady! How are you?"

"Better now."

He said, "Same here."

The weird feeling she hadn't been able to disentangle from, now made sense. Something in her psyche must've anticipated Jess's return and his lack of an I-missed-you vibe. "How'd things go with Alyssa?"

Jess looked down at his feet. "Let's just say my music is going to be put on hold for a while longer."

Elaina touched his arm. "She's not doing well?"

"Her anxieties go deeper than just breaking up with her boyfriend, having a spaced-out roomie, and taking classes that she's barely scraping by in." He puffed out a huge breath. "She's blaming her mother and I for her inability to get a decent night's sleep and for her failed relationships."

"That's not fair," erupted out of Elaina.

Jess's gaze snapped up. "You're right, it's not, but she needs me and I have to be there for her." He circled Elaina in an embrace.

Elaina laid her head on his shoulder. "You've come to collect your things."

Jess kissed her hair. "It's the last thing I want to do, Elaina." He set her back from him, but didn't let go. "I have some things I want to tell you. Please know that I'm a hundred percent sincere in what I say." He paused and then smiled. "The second you opened the door and our eyes met, I felt a strong pull. I'm so attracted to you, I can barely keep my hands where they belong, and frankly, I haven't felt that way about a woman since my divorce. I've wanted…and still want you in my bed."

Elaina trembled from the pleasure of those words, even though she knew a 'but' was coming.

"The more we connected on a cerebral level, the more I realized you were a woman who wouldn't be satisfied with just a tumble between the sheets. When you give your body, you also give your heart. Am I right?"

She pressed her lips together and nodded.

"Sad to say, but I'm not ready to accept anyone's heart – no matter how great they…you are."

There was that freaking 'but'. Elaina tried to keep her reaction from revealing the angst stirring inside. "Thanks for being honest, Jess."

"Remember when I said I thought I knew you from somewhere?"

"I remember."

"As corny as this is going to sound, I have to tell you that I definitely know you from somewhere." He lifted her chin so they were eye to eye. "I saw myself in you. I should say, I saw the person I used to be in you – hopeful, resilient, easy to give love and accept it, with mostly pure thoughts and a can-do attitude. I'm no longer that guy. I don't bounce back from heartache and letdowns. Like my daughter, I haven't dealt with some issues. Together, she and I are going to get to the bottom of the things holding us down and hopefully rise up from them." He ran his finger along her jaw line. "Being around you for a short time has been good for me. I've lost some weight," he lowered his voice to a more personal tone, "and you've restored in me the desire to be a better person. Someday when my head's in a better place, and if you're still single and want to see me, maybe we could take another trip together and actually spend the night in a hotel. I'm sorry we didn't stay in one on the way home from Ohio. I was afraid for us to spend the night together. Coming from a guy, that has to sound hokey but it's the truth, I swear."

Arden divorced her. Michael Rexx, the first guy she let into her life post-divorce went back to his wife and daughter. She spent some time with Chad Ferguson, who decided to permanently relocate to New York. And now Robert Jess Blakefield was saying arrivederci. Elaina wouldn't cry. Nope. No way would she shed tears for what wasn't meant to be. Damn. All this not-meant-to-be crap was getting old. She couldn't help but wonder if one night of passion with Jess would've changed the outcome for them. "I believe you, Jess. I hate for you to leave, but your daughter has to be your main concern." Those were almost the same words she'd said to Michael Rexx when he decided to reunite with his family.

"Elaina, I told Alyssa I'd be back to Virginia after you and I drive the coast."

"You and I talked at length about your mother's fascination with the sea. I'd like to help you get an answer as to why she loved it so much."

"You can't delay the much needed healing for Alyssa and for you."

"Are you afraid I'll jump your bones and then leave?"

I'm afraid you won't jump them. Elaina gave him an impish grin and avoided the question with a question. "You'd really drive with me up the coast to help satisfy my curiosity?"

"I said I would one other time. I meant it. Of course, it'll be a day trip. We'll drive on Route 1 for eight hours and then turn around. What do you say?"

"Let's do it."

* * *

Grace eyed Elaina. "You're okay with him leaving?"

"I don't have a choice. I have to be okay with it."

"You DO have a choice. You can tell him how you feel. If you're as into him as I think you are, he should be told."

"I have to do the right thing and not make a scene."

"Are you buying this BS, ladies?" Grace looked at Tawny and Steph, who were sitting at the table with them in the sunroom for their Wednesday night wine club.

"No," Tawny said forcefully.

"Hell no," Steph said with even more energy.

"I'm a no, too. Let's recap: we have two no's and one hell no. For once in your life, Elaina, put yourself first and give him a reason to stay. Tomorrow morning while you're driving north, slide your hand up his thigh and bat those sexy eyelashes."

"We might wreck." Elaina laughed and blackberry wine sloshed out of her glass.

Grace groaned. "Your turn, Tawn'."

"Grace is right, you know. You take care of other people's hearts and neglect your own. Be wild and reckless. Carpe diem his fine ass."

Steph's brows bumped together. "Seize the day his fine ass? That doesn't make sense."

"In order to win Jess, I have to jump HIS bones?"

"Exactly."

"What about Alyssa?"

Tawny slapped a hand to her forehead. "More wine, Grace."

Grace poured Tawny's glass half full.

"Ut, ut. What's this half glass crap?"

Steph kicked Elaina's foot under the table. "They want you to have sex with Jess, which will either fix what ails you or complicate them to the point you'll be glad he moved to Virginia. I'm not endorsing their suggestions, but I want you to be happy. If sex will do the trick, then have at it."

"Having sex with someone I barely know scares me to my bone marrow."

"Stop over-thinking and dissecting every move you

make. Your pulse goes up and your thighs quiver when you see Jess." Tawny peered over the rim of her glass. "Right?"

"My thighs don't quiver."

"Liar, liar, thighs on fire."

"Tawn', you know how I am. I'm going to forfeit a night of pleasure for the greater good. The greater good is Alyssa. Besides, I'd rather be wild and reckless with the three of you. Let's snowboard. If we survive, then we'll make a pilgrimage back to Ohio."

"For what, may I ask?"

"We took off out of there without tying up loose ends."

Tawny, Steph, and Grace looked at one another.

Tawny slurped wine and smacked her lips. "Loose ends?"

"I haven't pinpointed anything specific, but there has to be some."

Grace twirled her finger around her ear. "Someone at this table is cuckoo. I'm going to carpe diem your wine until you admit what's really at play here." She moved Elaina's glass to the far end of the table.

Elaina sat up from a slouch. "Since we set foot in our bed and breakfast, we've all had doubts and episodes of adjustment. Clearly the fault is mine. I pressured you into coming here and it threw our lives into lockdown."

"You might as well be speaking French, because I'm not getting what you're trying to say."

"When we met, we had fun. We did the cha-cha at that nightclub. We sang karaoke, badly, but we still did it. We spent time in the hot tub. You put purple streaks in your hair, Grace, and we all got infinity tattoos on our ankles. You talked about getting a nipple ring. I'm glad you didn't. The point I'm trying to make is that we did things. Now that we're here, we've become homebodies."

"You might be a stuffed hen, I'm not." Grace wagged her finger. "It's winter. It's normal not to venture out as much. When the weather's great, it'll be hard to stay inside." She lifted her ankle high for everyone to see. "I'm proud to wear this tattoo, because you're my besties forever. I wouldn't mind getting another one. Are you game?"

Elaina hesitated.

"You want to rev things up, right?"

"Not with ink."

"I give up. Steph, we've tried to penetrate that dense forest in her head. The trees are just too thick. Do you have anything sharp to clear a few branches?"

Steph drummed her fingers on the table. "The best thing about being together is how we help each other step out of our comfort zones. Lately, we've settled in. I'm not sure that was our intention, but it's an easy trap to fall into. You're right, Elaina, none of us want to become crotchedy old hens. We're intelligent women with a fighting spirit and a sense of adventure. We also worry way too much. Those anxieties don't make us weak; they make us human and keep us humble."

"Thank you for that, Steph." Elaina looked at Grace and Tawny. "She gets me." A long sigh rolled out. "It's confession time. I've been struggling with this newfound freedom known as being single. It's great; at the same time it's no walk in the park. I love being able to make my own decisions, yet I question if I'm making the right ones."

Tawny agreed with a nod. "It's a day-to-day challenge. Each of us went from two people working toward our destinies, down to one."

Grace refilled their glasses. "We didn't go down to one – we went up by three. I get your message though, Elaina. We're single, not by choice, but now that we are we have to adopt a – look out world mindset. I've wanted to snowboard, so that's going to happen. Our guest register is currently lacking reservations. Instead of freaking out about it, let's shake things up and do things. If what the locals say is true, we'll be so busy when tourist season starts that we won't have a chance to sit down until November."

"All in favor of Elaina having sex with Jess…" Tawny threw her hand in the air, followed by Grace and Steph. "All in favor of shaking up our lives." Four hands joined above the table.

Grace was out of her chair and out of the sunroom in a heartbeat. She returned with an armful of jackets. "We're going to seal this new pledge with something special."

"This can't be good."

"Erring on the side of caution is what normal people do." Tawny slid her arms into a denim jacket and wrapped a fuzzy scarf around her neck. "Semi-normal is as good as it gets around here."

* * *

"Ouch, ouch, ouch."

"Hold still or yours is going to say One of Four Sassy Chi's, instead of Chicks." Grace crossed her arms.

"Getting our ankles tattooed was one thing; getting the tender skin above our breast is something altogether different."

"Don't think of it as above your breast. Think of it as over your heart."

"Breast, heart, whatever. The sucker hurts."

Ben, their tattoo artist ignored Steph's whining and their pleas for each other to suck it up. He was laser focused and continued his art with a steady hand.

"I may pass out."

"I'd advise you to stay conscious. You could wake up with a nipple ring."

"Two can play that game. The next time I cook and you take your first bite, ask yourself if you should."

Ben finally intervened. "Ladies, be nice. I can't work under these conditions."

One by one, they apologized.

"Thank you. Now give Steph your support and we'll be good to go."

"Steph, you've got this. Take a deep breath and relax."

Steph followed Elaina's instructions. She inhaled, exhaled, and closed her eyes.

In just their bras, Elaina, Tawny, and Grace stood in front of the mirror and admired the ink.

"I love this." Tawny struck a few poses to see the tattoo from every angle.

Awe gushed from Grace.

"The script font is classy and the tiny anchor at the end..." Elaina got choked up. "It's perfect."

"With my eyes closed, it sounds like he's about to saw me in half."

Ben stopped the tattoo machine, put his hand over his eyes, and shook his head.

"Place the blame on Elaina. This was her idea."

"I beg your pardon. Grace drove here without telling us where we were headed. I had nothing in it."

Tawny patted Elaina on the back. "Indirectly you're to blame for a lot of things."

"I'm not to blame for that pea-green bra you're wearing. Where'd you get that thing? The Jolly Green Giant's gift shop?" Elaina jokingly rubbed her eyes.

Grace bumped Tawny with her elbow. "The train is back on the tracks – we're mouthy and misbehaving in public, we're parading around without our shirts, and people will home in on our chests to read our new tattoo."

Chapter Fourteen

~ And now you know! ~

"Are you ready?" Jess smiled from the driver's seat.

After all that talk about quivering thighs and sleeping with Jess, Elaina couldn't look him in the eyes. "I've got my seatbelt fastened, Captain."

The warmth of his smile made her squinch her legs together.

"Even if you don't get the answer you seek, you'll love the trip. I drive Route 1 every summer. Usually, I'm by myself. My ex and daughter did it once with me and they didn't care to do it again. I just don't get that. The scenery is breathtaking, and if you allow it, it becomes part of your soul."

"You're very deep," Elaina said softly.

"That's debatable, but I know how the coast makes me feel." Jess slipped a pair of sunglasses on his nose. "The snow's melting, the sun's shining, and we're going to explore for about six hours. It's eight o'clock right now. At two this afternoon, we have to turn around to get back to familiar territory by dark. The early sunsets make winter seem that much longer."

"It doesn't matter how long we're gone. I'm just tickled that we're going."

Jess headed down Baxter Boulevard and onto I-295/Route 1. "Did you know that Portland is the foodie capital of Maine?"

"I did not. I'll have to tell Steph."

"You might also like to know that Portland Head Light is America's first lighthouse. It was commissioned by George Washington to guard Maine's busiest harbor." He snickered. "No wonder Alyssa isn't keen on taking this drive with me, I turn into a history book."

"Suggest it to her again. I'm sure she'll jump at the chance." Elaina studied the atlas that lay in her lap. "Only a local can provide the special nuances that someone traveling here from out of state isn't privy to. Please, Jess, be my passionate tour guide."

"Happy to oblige, milady."

Elaina placed her arm on the console and Jess laid his next to hers so they touched.

"There are three primary coastal regions. If you want sandy beaches, you go to Southern Maine. If you prefer rocky, go Mid-coast. In the DownEast section you'll find rugged bluffs. Each region offers something special." He explained that in DownEast the ocean tides are some of the highest on the planet, with high and low tides occurring twice a day.

"This is great."

"I knew you'd like it."

Elaina ran her fingers back and forth over the anchor charm on her necklace. *I'm here, Mom.*

They stopped at each quaint little town, some for only five minutes.

In Rockland, they stopped for Lobster Eggs Benedict.

Elaina took one bite and said, "Mmm. This is delicious! I have to take a picture for Steph."

"Wait until you taste goat cheese and blackberry ice cream." As soon as it was out of his mouth, he said he'd only get one scoop. He ran a hand over his stomach, "Less paunch now. Thanks to you."

A half hour later, they got out of the car to stretch their legs again.

Standing on the jutting rocks along the shore, Elaina breathed in the salty air. Wind whipped through her hair and cold permeated her layers of clothing. She snuggled close to Jess to get warm. Without any forethought, the disquiet surrounding her heart turned into words. "How can you leave all this, Jess?"

"I'm only leaving temporarily, just until Alyssa and I feel whole again."

"Would Alyssa consider moving back to Maine and attend the University of New England – Portland?"

"We discussed it. She's not on board with the idea at this time." Jess took Elaina's hand and brought it to his lips and began to sing, A LITTLE BIT MORE by Dr. Hook.

The lyrics sent her over the edge, luckily not over the cliff to hang on a tree like she did with Stone-man. "We have to go NOW."

Jess dropped her hand. "What's wrong?"

"Nothing. Everything." She came close to adding, "My thighs are quivering."

"You're the boss."

"No I'm not. If I were the boss..." Elaina let the thought unfinished.

"If you were the boss, what?"

She sifted air through her teeth. "I can't say. It's inappropriate."

"Whisper it then."

Elaina touched his ear with her lips and quietly shared what she'd like to do.

"I thought you'd never ask."

Like two love-starved teenagers, they ran to the car and headed back to Rockland.

On the balcony of the hotel room overlooking the harbor, with Jess's arms wrapped around her from behind, Elaina stared out at the water for the longest time. She turned and kissed Jess until they were both out of air. With the crashing of waves in the background and three quarters of a moon shining overhead, a peace unlike any she'd ever known took her over. "This was the perfect day."

"It's going to get even better."

* * *

"I tried to call you several times last night." Tawny stood with her hands on her hips. "My calls kept going to voicemail. The text you sent stating you'd see us in the morning wasn't enough."

Elaina slung her purse on the counter. "I'll be back to answer all your questions as soon as I'm finished calling my aunt Vernene."

"Your aunt in Seattle?"

"Uh huh." Elaina rushed out of the kitchen and headed toward the basement. Over her shoulder, she heard Grace say, "Do I detect a spring in her step?" Grace laughed when Steph said, "Boing! Boing!"

In the privacy of her basement bedroom, she made the call. Vernene answered on the first ring.

"Dear girl, it's so good to hear from you. You've been on my mind a lot lately."

"I'm sorry it's been so long since we've spoken." Elaina made small talk with her mom's sister for a good hour. They talked about the bed and breakfast, and the mild winter in Seattle versus the more harsh winter in Maine. Vernene was a retired Political Science professor, so she briefly touched on politics.

"I can't stop smiling, Aunt Vernene. You sound so much like Mom."

"That warms my heart, Elaina. I miss her so much and I know you do too."

Another twenty missed passed with them reliving memories of great times together.

"That Luther Vandross concert was wonderful. I'm glad we went. I still have my t-shirt. I can't believe someone your age actually wanted your folks and your spinster aunt to go with you."

"We had the best time, didn't we? I still have my t-shirt

too. I've worn it so much you can read the newspaper through it. I think it's time to frame it or toss it." Elaina heard Roxie, her aunt's Shih Tzu barking to get attention.

Aunt Vernene tried unsuccessfully to shush Roxie. "I have to go, Elaina. Roxie is turning in circles. If I don't take her outside soon, she'll get mad and tinkle on the carpet."

"Before I hang up, I have something important to ask. Mom was so in love with the sea and I've been on a quest to find out why. Can you shed some light on it?"

A warm laugh filtered through the phone line. "You keyed on the answer with your comment about your mom. It all centers on love. Your mom may or may not have told you the difficulty she had getting pregnant."

Elaina sat on the edge of the bed. "I asked her several times over the years why I was an only child. All she'd say was we were meant to be a family of three."

"That is so your mom. When she didn't want to give a direct answer, she didn't. But you're getting one now. Your mom and dad tried everything short of surrogacy to have a baby. Nothing worked. Your father had a slew of tests done too. The doctors couldn't explain why they couldn't get pregnant. All their parts seemed to be in working order. They eventually gave up. To distract themselves from the hurt, they booked a cruise. Somewhere between the Virgin Islands and St. Kitts, you were conceived. In my mind, it was a relaxation thing. After you were born, they tried to have another child and ran into the same difficulty. They were so thankful to have been blessed with you. You're the reason she loved the sea, Elaina."

Unexpected emotion streamed from Elaina's eyes. "Thank you for sharing that with me, Aunt Vernene. I needed to know."

Roxie went spastic, and she and her aunt were forced to end the call.

Elaina savored the information and swiped at the happiness leaking from her eyes. "I've said it before and now I know it's true, you've led me here, Mom. Did you also lead me to Jess?" She ran up the basement steps.

Tawny cut in front of her when she got to the kitchen. "I thought you'd never wrap up the call to your aunt."

Elaina gave Tawny a half hug. "Our discussion has to be put on hold a little while longer." She sidestepped her friend and dashed out of the house and to the loft.

Jess answered the door dressed in his coat and hat, with a box of his belongings in his arms. He sat the box aside. "Everything okay?"

"I know we've said our goodbyes, but there's something I have to tell you."

He guided her to the sofa. "What is it?"

Elaina wet her lips and began, "You've made it clear that you aren't ready to give your heart to anyone. I was at that same place too. The thought of giving everything of myself to someone again, scared the heck out of me." She put his hand on her chest and held it there. "I met you and something clicked into place."

"Are you saying you fell in love with me?"

"I think that's what I'm trying to say. I thought you should know."

Jess had been around them long enough to pick up

on their random facts quirkiness and when to use it. "And you should know there are fault lines in Maine."

"That explains why the earth moves every time we kiss."

* * *

Elaina returned to the house to find a chair sitting in the middle of the floor. "What have we here?"

"Your interrogation chair, have a seat."

"No thank you."

Tawny hollered for assistance from Grace and Steph.

"Ah ha! The wayward mistress has returned."

Elaina put her butt in the chair. "Wayward mistress. Pfft. You're the one who wanted to be naughty, not me."

"Yet you're the one who has embraced the fun of it."

"Jess and I were tired. We decided to bunk in Rockland for the night."

Tawny raised her eyebrows. "Malarkey."

"Double malarkey," Steph added.

All eyes zipped to Steph.

"You're a bit of a nerd," Grace quipped.

"But you're an amazing cook. Did you know Portland is the foodie capital of Maine?"

"You already told me that via a text."

Tawny anchored a hand on her hip. "Steph, get a shovel. Elaina's going to make us dig for information. Better yet, get a jackhammer. We'll chip away at her resistance until she tells us every juicy morsel."

"No shovels are needed. Fortunately, we have no

jackhammers." Elaina modestly cleared her throat and pulled back her shoulders. "There's nothing to tell, really. We drove the coast, ate some incredible food, spooned all night long, and here I am – back to bug you all day."

Tawny and Grace traded amused looks.

"You're leaving out the creamy center." Steph jabbed Grace in the shoulder. "And no, creamy center is not a double entendre."

"Just when you think Steph doesn't have a clue, she zings us."

Elaina stuck up for Steph. "She always has a clue."

"Sweet talk won't lessen the cross-examination."

"See? She knows exactly what's going on."

"Enough stalling, wayward woman." Grace took a pocket-size flashlight from the junk drawer and flicked it on. She shined it at Elaina. "Did you or did you not have coitus with Jess?"

"We made love, sort of."

"I knew it! Wait. What?" Grace looked befuddled. "How do you sort of have sex?"

"I didn't use the word sex, I said made love. Tawn', I saw you roll your eyes." Elaina wrung her hands in her lap, stretched her neck from side to side, and twisted her hips to the right and to the left. "This is actually between me and Jess."

"You can't dangle a carrot and then pull it back."

Elaina blew out a breath. "Jess and I didn't have the whole lovemaking experience."

"Oh brother! I need wine."

"Tawn', it's ten-thirty in the morning." Elaina started

to leave the chair and was held in place by Grace.

"Anytime is a good time for wine."

Elaina sniffed the air and glanced to where a Crock pot was plugged in. "You made hot mulled wine?"

Steph's cheeks rose with a high smile. "To celebrate you finally getting some."

"I didn't get some."

Grace flicked the flashlight off and on in warning. "We need a lie detector home-edition."

Elaina chewed on her bottom lip. "I'm forty-four. I don't have to put up with this crap."

"You made love, but didn't have the whole lovemaking experience. You're toying with us. Just spill your guts all ready."

"Geez. Peer pressure galore." Elaina cupped her mouth and lowered her voice to make it sound like she was sharing the details of a covert operation. "Here's how it went down."

Tawny whapped her on the arm. "In your boss voice, please."

"HERE'S HOW IT WENT DOWN."

"I'm ordering pizza. We're going to be here for a while." Grace grabbed the phone book.

Elaina put up her palms. "Jess and I engaged in some light foreplay. He was ready to take it to the next level and so was I. Then Alyssa called."

"Huge buzzkill," Steph chirped.

"Alyssa and her dad talked for an hour."

"Hard to recapture the moment?"

"Exactly." Elaina smiled, remembering Jess's touch.

"Why the mad dash out to the loft?"
"I had to tell him I loved him."
You could've heard a pin drop.

Chapter Fifteen

~ Even monkeys need an occasional surprise! ~

"Stony's mad about something. He won't come to me. All he does is lay there staring into space."

"Maybe he's sick." Elaina stopped unloading the dishwasher.

"I lifted his eyelids. His eyes don't look funky. His nose is cold and wet. I don't think he's sick."

Elaina stacked clean plates in the cabinet. "He's probably not getting enough exercise. I haven't taken him on as many walks as I usually do."

"That's because it's been nasty outside. Grace had all ready given us heart failure by falling. We don't want the same thing to happen with you skidding out of control. Stone-man is just going to have to deal with the weather, just like us."

"You don't think he misses Lula, do you?"

There was a glimmer of possibility in Tawny's brown eyes. "You might be on to something. Let's do a test." She motioned for Elaina to follow. They found him in

Tawny's bedroom curled up in his bed. Bailey had her nose jammed in his side. "Are you missing Lula?"

Stony perked.

"You are a smart woman, Elaina Samuels. You've diagnosed the problem." Tawny and Elaina trekked to the stairway. "Nick, you got a minute?"

Nicholas leaned over the banister. "What's up, gals?"

"Do you know if Norma is working right now?"

"It's six-ish. She should be off the clock."

"Excellent. Thank you, my good man."

Nicholas chuckled. "You four women are a treat." He started to return to Steph's room, but stopped. "By the way, Norma's been a godsend. She works her butt off and gets along well with the staff. That frees me up to be with Steph. You did good, Elaina."

Elaina saluted him.

Tawny inquired how the cookbook was coming.

"It's half finished."

"Can we have a look-see sometime?"

Steph heard the question and popped out of the bedroom. "No you may not. Did Leonardo da Vinci show The Last Supper at the halfway mark? No he didn't. Did J. K. Rowling share a few chapters before the first Harry Potter book was finished? I think not. Did Francis Ford Coppola tease the viewing public by letting them see the first half of The Godfather prior to the film's completion?"

"I believe the answer is no."

Steph laughed herself back into the bedroom.

Nicholas shrugged and disappeared too.

Elaina sent Norma a text. *'Stony needs a Lula-fix. Can we come over?'*

Norma replied, *'Sure. Lula will be thrilled.'*

Elaina then fired off a text to Grace. *'We're headed to Norma's so Stony can bother Lula for an hour or so. Want to join us?'*

A few minutes passed without a reply.

"She and Philip are probably at the halfway mark of NOT having the full lovemaking experience."

"Ha. You're a laugh a minute. Should we wait to hear from her?"

"It might take a while for them to finish what they're NOT doing."

Elaina gave her the stink eye. "Come on, Stone-man. We're off to visit the cat you used to ignore but now miss."

Stony came running and couldn't get stopped in time. He knocked over a floor lamp. Elaina sprung into action and caught the lamp before it crashed to the floor. "I'd say he's excited."

Tawny shouted for Steph to keep an eye on Bailey while they were gone.

In Elaina's SUV, the sweet pooch pressed his nose against the back passenger window, leaving a huge nose print on the glass. He went to the opposite window and did the same thing.

Tawny rapped her knuckles on Norma's door. She greeted Norma with a hug. Switching from her regular voice to cartoony for Lula, she said, "Hello, Shredder."

Lula hunkered close to Norma's legs, not particularly

interested in their presence. Her nose and whiskers twitched, sniffing the air until she caught a whiff of Stony. She said hello to him in cat-speak with a series of meows. Stony threw his head up and yowled with delight. Norma could barely close the door with the two animals trying to get at each other.

To their surprise, Lula didn't dart under anything to hide. She even left Norma's shadow to repeatedly swat a paw at Stony. Stony arched his back and moved back like he was scared. Then he'd advance on her again.

Elaina marveled at the difference in their actions. "Would you look at those two? When they were together in Ohio and then when we moved to the bed and breakfast, they behaved as if the other was an inconvenience. Now they're long lost buddies."

"I've worked with people like that over the years. The moment they put their waitress' apron on, they became temperamental, territorial, and inflexible. If I'd see them at the grocery or anywhere else outside of work, they'd go out of their way to be nice."

"Maybe they were cats in another life."

"Tawny, you have a wicked sense of humor."

"I get it from Elaina."

They laughed.

"I know you try to eat healthy, but I made a sugar cream pie earlier. Would you like a piece?"

"Celery and carrots are overrated. Bring on the pie." Tawny rubbed her hands together.

"How is Steph doing with her diet?"

"She's done great. Once in a while she'll cheat with

something decadent, but she goes back to low-cal. She's down a pants size."

"Since she loves to cook, I imagine her temptation to stray is difficult."

"It's easy to forget that, Norma. Tawn', we have to stop complaining when she creates dishes with sauerkraut."

"I loooove sauerkraut."

"You also loooove that crazy cat."

Norma almost had a bite of pie to her mouth. The fork shook from her laughter and the chunk of pie dislodged from the tines and found the floor.

Stony beat Lula to the mishap and gulped it down before she had a chance at it. The battle was on. Lula hissed and her claws came out.

"Lula doesn't have a tiny apron on, but she's temperamental, territorial, and inflexible."

For the briefest of moments, a frown creased Norma's forehead.

Tawny backpedaled. "This is her home and that was her scrap of pie. Bad dog, Stone-man."

Stony cocked his head at the reprimand.

Norma jumped up from the table and took a foil pack of cat treats from the pantry. "Come here, sweet girl."

Lula was putty in Norma's hands, for more reasons than just a tuna-flavored treat.

"You have a way with animals, Norma."

"I can be firm, but mostly I shower them with attention and the end result is unconditional love."

"Kind of like how you are with us, Elaina."

Elaina gave Tawny a shove and almost pushed her off

the chair. Stony came over to protect his mistress. He looked at Tawny and then at Elaina. "She deserved it, Stony. I swear."

Tawny stroked the velvet of his ears.

"There's your unconditional love, Tawn'. Stony's fond of me and he's knows I'm not a threat to you. But if he sensed I meant to do real harm he'd rip into me."

Tawny knelt and wrapped her arms around Stony.

Norma put Lula in her lap. "People may fail us, but animals never do."

When it was time to go, they stood and Lula knew what was happening. She jumped at Stony and took off across the living room. Stony set chase again.

"Some things never change."

Stony leaped over an ottoman and pushed against the coffee table in an effort to get the cat.

"Stony, you're too big to run inside. You'll wreck Norma's condo. Give Lula a kiss and let's go."

Lula ran under a lamp table to tease Stony.

Tawny latched Stone-man's leash on his collar.

The click brought Lula out from under the furniture. She brushed up against Stony several times. Stony put a paw on her and poked her with his snout.

"Do you suppose that's a kiss?"

"Probably. That's how Jess and Elaina do it."

Elaina grabbed a handful of Tawny's hair, but didn't pull it. "Make another wisecrack. I dare you."

Norma quirked a grin. "Now I know where Lula gets it."

* * *

"The realtor is going to show us the house today."

Tawny pulled the comforter up around her. "Grace it's eight-thirty. I'm trying to sleep here."

"The world starts turning before eight-thirty."

"I'm well aware, but I'm scheduled for a twelve-hour shift tonight at the hospital. I need to catch some extra Zzz's."

"You can't store sleep."

"Not with you nagging, I can't." Tawny buried her face in the pillow.

Elaina stood in the doorway with a cup of coffee, watching the tussle.

Tawny caught her presence. "A little help?"

"Grace, let her be. We'll check out the eighteenth century house without her."

Tawny raised her head with a grimace on her face. "You can't go without me."

"Then get your keister up."

Stony was yowling from the kitchen like mad and Bailey was yipping right along with him.

"What's their deal?" Tawny grumbled.

Elaina scratched her back on the door jamb. "They want to be taken out."

"That isn't Stony's business yowl."

"Then you should probably get up and find out what's got him so worked up."

"Steph is probably teasing him and Bailey with ham." Tawny threw back the covers, slung her feet to the floor, and griped that everyone was so freaking cheery in the morning and it needed to stop. "Couldn't you wait an hour or so before turning into happy-go-lucky morning persons? Nooooo, you could not. The moment your feet hit the floor you sing and laugh."

"Pancakes are ready."

Grace threw a decorative pillow and it hit Tawny in the chest. "Don't dilly dally or I'll eat them all."

"You have a mean streak, Grace Vivian."

"So you've said on many occasions."

"I speaketh the truth."

Grace backed out of the room, most likely anticipating a retaliatory pillow throw. "You complain about it being early, yet you're lucid enough to quote Shakespeare."

"That's not Shakespeare." Elaina sipped her coffee and smacked her lips.

Tawny wanted to know what part she got wrong.

"All of it."

Grace and Elaina met up with Steph in the kitchen. "Did you tell her?"

"We said we wouldn't."

Tawny clomped out of her bedroom, still dressed in her pajamas and sporting ankle-high boots on her feet. Her hair looked like she'd been zapped by electricity. Halfway across the living room, she put her arms straight out and walked toward them like a zombie. In a deep, gravelly voice she said, "I need coffee."

Another deep, gravelly voice said, "I'll get you a cup."

Tawny stopped dead in her tracks.

Bo and Quentin popped out of the kitchen with huge

smiles plastered on their faces. "Mornin', Mom."

Her surprised and confused gaze jetted from her sons to Grace. "You didn't just bug me to see your house, you were also trying to get me to come out to see my boys."

"I did a mighty fine job, if I do say so myself."

Tawny ran to Bo and Quentin. They squeezed her in their arms. "How? Why? I'm so happy to see you."

"We missed you."

Over Bo's shoulder, Tawny searched for Elaina. "You summoned them?"

Elaina didn't know whether to smile or run for cover. "Maybe."

The doorbell rang.

"That's probably Philip. He can't wait to see the house."

Steph said it could be Bart. "He's been missing in action for over a week."

Tawny's happy face fell just a little. "You're right."

Whoever was at the door repeatedly pushed the button. Ding dong sounded at least a dozen times.

"Give a girl a chance to get there." Grace yanked open the door. She went slack and teetered backward. She turned with shock etched in every speck of her face. "Elainaaaa?"

"Not Bart?" Elaina asked.

"You know the answer." Grace mouthed the words, "Thank you."

Looking as handsome as ever, was her son Cody – Brince's mini-me. "Hi, Mom."

Grace steepled her hands over her mouth and nose,

and tears cascaded down her cheeks. "I can't believe you're here."

Cody picked Grace up. "You're such a tiny thing. Are you eating enough?"

"Yes," she replied softly.

Steph vouched for her. "She's no slacker when it comes to pancakes. I made enough for all of you."

Philip showed up when there were two pancakes left. "This is a great day." He shook Cody's hand and pecked Grace on the forehead.

Excitement filled the bed and breakfast, with everyone talking at once.

Elaina excused herself, scooped up Bailey, and went into the bathroom with her phone. She smiled when she found a picture Jess had sent. It was a selfie of he and Alyssa. He was grinning like a Cheshire cat and holding up a stalk of celery. Alyssa was pointing to the vegetable and sticking out her tongue. His message read: *I'm making 'Lyss eat better. I miss you.*

A knock on the bathroom door made Elaina close her email app. "Yeah?"

"Is everything okay?"

"It's better than okay, Grace."

* * *

"We don't want to overwhelm the realtor." Philip surveyed the amount of people who'd donned coats to check out the house. "Only half of you can come at one time."

Bo grinned. "My top half will go first."

Quentin ribbed his brother. "I'm not carrying you across the street."

"The apples didn't fall far from the tree, Tawn'."

"Elaina, you knew I needed those apples in a big way. How'd you pull it off? They have jobs."

Bo answered for Elaina. "She put this in motion shortly after Christmas."

Grace asked the same question about Cody.

He nodded. "She wanted Isabella and Karina to come as well, but it didn't work out this time. Karina wanted me to give you this." It was a hand-drawn card. Cody, Isabella, and Karina were stick people with speech balloons that said 'Buon Compleanno!' "That's Happy Birthday in Italian, Mom. It's a few days early, but I thought you'd like to have it now."

Grace gingerly touched the card. "I love you guys." She opened the card and read the message inside. It was written in crayon and in Italian. Below in Isabella's handwriting, the same thought was written in English. Grace's voice cracked with emotion as she read it out loud. "It's signed, Love to you, from Cody, Isabella, and Karina. P.S. Sorry Karina and I couldn't make it this trip. I've been having a lot of morning sickness." She slapped a hand over her mouth. "Does this mean what I think it means?"

Cody lifted her up and swung her around. "Congratulations, Grandma Grace."

Grace cried and laughed. She was a happy, blubbering mess and so was everyone else.

Cody tenderly said, "It's the reason we're staying in Italy – for now. Eventually, we'll all be moving here."

Philip placed a hand on Cody's shoulder. "There's a big house, just waiting to be filled."

"Are you serious? Isabella's parents plan to join us. You'd have the whole clan."

"La mia casa e la tua casa."

Cody interpreted, "My house is your house."

Grace blinked up at Philip with adoration. "You speak Italian?"

"A little."

"No wonder I love you."

It was Philip's turn to be shocked. He drew back with a huge smile. "You love me?"

"Haven't you been paying attention?"

Philip kissed the tip of Grace's nose. He probably would've given her a bigger kiss but he had a full audience. "I love you, too."

Tawny was on her game and used the same line Grace had used on her a while back. "Get a room."

"How about several?" Philip took Grace's hand. "We have an antique to look at and buy."

"Check me out all you want, I'm not for sale."

"Good one, Mom." Bo hip-checked Tawny.

Steph inquired about the pilgrimage. "Are we still headed to Ohio?"

"I thought we needed to go back, but it appears we're good. Besides, who has the time? We're going to snowboard and ski and get into all kinds of mischief here."

Quentin pumped a fist in the air. "Yes! I can't wait to snowboard. Can we go later today?"

Realization dawned and Tawny's happy look faded to sad. "I have to work."

"No you don't."

"I'm on the schedule, Elaina."

"No you're not."

Those silky brown brows lifted. "Don't toy with me."

"I knew when your boys were coming and talked to your nursing supervisor to arrange for you to have the week off."

"Because I do PRN, she texted me yesterday to confirm I'd be there today."

"She played her part well."

"I harp at you for over-thinking things. What you're actually doing is thinking everything through."

"And she's hot!" Bo gave Elaina a licentious grin.

"I'm tepid at best."

Bo negated her assessment. "Hot and humble! Do you date younger guys?"

Tawny backhanded him on the chest. "Hit on somebody your own age."

"Forgive me, Elaina. I was out of line." He winked.

Philip pointed south. "To the antique we go."

The house Philip and Grace considered buying looked rough on the outside from a lack of care. It was missing a few scalloped shingles and some slats in the wooden wrap-around porch were spongy. Paint on the ornamental spindles had peeled. Inside the house was a different story. The foyer had a winding staircase made of cherry that looked like it had been recently renovated. Textured walls were in good shape, as well as the hardwood floors. Elaina fell in love with the front parlor. The stone fireplace was huge and a large bay-type window had a paisley padded seat. Normally she wasn't fond of mustard colored paint, in that room it worked.

"It has a library!" Grace squealed. "Look at all the shelves."

The realtor smiled and encouraged them to peruse the place at their leisure.

Elaina whispered to Grace, "Tone down the excitement or they won't budge on the price."

Steph went gaga over the kitchen. She ran a hand over the black stove made of cast-iron. "It has an old, authentic look, but it's fairly new. Be still my heart." Her fingertips touched everything. "It's short on cabinets, but notice the wooden slots on the far wall. I presume that's to tuck plates in. Get a load of this table and the low beam above it. I can picture copper cookware hanging from hooks."

"Philip, we have an interior decorator at our disposal."

"I only do kitchens. You'll have to snag Tawny for the rest of the place."

"She did do a great job purchasing the purple beast." Grace gave Elaina a cheesy grin.

"Whatever."

Tawny came up from the basement. "It's creepy down there. On the plus side, it has a walk-out door. How cool is that?"

The realtor spoke up. "By creepy, you mean authentic.

The owners wanted to keep as many things actual to the time period as they could."

"No, I mean creepy."

The realtor's expression flared with displeasure, but she recovered quickly and posed a question to Philip and Grace. "What do you think? Is this place for you?"

Philip rubbed his chin. "It has character, but it needs a phenomenal amount of work."

"Most homes with any history to them do."

"We have another group that has to check it out. Then you, me, and Grace will talk money. Afterward, we're going snowboarding. This evening we'll invite everyone to voice their opinions. Grace and I will call you in the morning with our decision."

The realtor's confident veneer cracked a little. "You're going to let all these people weigh in with their opinions?"

"We're one big happy family. Of course, we want their opinions."

Elaina put her fist out for Philip to knuckle bump. "No wonder Grace loves you."

* * *

Quentin assumed the lead role for snowboarding. "Melinda and I have snowboarded numerous times."

"How's she doing?"

A sheepish grin washed into Quentin's expression. "She just might be the one."

Tawny glowed with pride. "Keep me informed." She'd met Melinda on her trek out west a few months earlier. When she returned home, she was giddy with excitement for her son and hoped one day he'd get down on one knee and ask Melinda to marry him.

"Mom, I talked to one of the guy's in the lodge. They put on a snowboarding camp here from February through March. You ladies should look into it." Quentin commenced giving information to get them started. "Skiing is actually easier to learn, but harder to master; whereas, snowboarding is more difficult to grasp, but easier to do. That may not make sense now, but once we get started you'll see what I'm talking about." He took them to a beginner's slope and demonstrated the proper way to stop. "I should back up and give you a few basic rules. First and foremost, choose your route ahead of time. It's easier to navigate, if you know where you're headed. Control your speed. Be careful when overtaking other boarders. Give them a wide berth and plenty of respect."

Bo teased his brother. "Saying 'Get out of my way, fool,' is wrong?"

Quentin tilted his head in a mock. "You won't have to worry about the boarder giving you a black eye afterward, I'll give you one."

"Catch me if you can. I'm lightning on my feet."

Quentin surprised Bo with a push that put his butt in the snow and those lightning feet in the air.

Bo pulled to a stand. "People, respect other boarders."

"You're such a goon. Let's get back to learning how to snowboard." Quentin showed them the proper posture. "Stand with your entire body facing downhill and your board against the incline."

Steph shouted, "Woohoo! I can't wait!"

Tawny feigned astonishment. "This coming from the woman who was scared the tattoo guy was going to saw her in half?"

Bo's eyebrow shot up. "You got another tattoo?"

Steph grinned. "We all did. I have too many clothes on at the moment or I'd show you."

"Mom?"

"It's Elaina's fault."

Elaina broke into a side-splitting laugh.

The big shock of the day and most heartwarming moment came when Cody said he wanted no part of snowboarding because he was a husband to Isabella, a dad to Karina, and he didn't want to be in a body cast when the baby arrived. "I can't risk getting hurt."

Chapter Sixteen

- Friends forever, no time or distance can separate! -

A week later, the house was back to just Elaina, Tawny, Steph and Nick, Grace, and the pooches. Bo and Quentin had hugged their mom and said, 'I love you' a zillion times. They also promised to call and text more often. Cody had a hard time leaving Grace; at the same time he couldn't wait to get back to his family and their baby-to-be. Grace vowed to fly to Italy to be there for the birth. Steph and Nick added some Italian recipes to their cookbook, in Cody's honor. Elaina continued to get daily updates from Jess. In one of his messages, he said Alyssa couldn't wait to meet her. In the same communiqué he mentioned it would be a while before it happened.

Prior to everyone going their separate ways, Grace and Philip made an offer on the house and the owner accepted. Closing was to take place mid-March. At Nicholas's recommendation they celebrated Grace's birthday and Valentine's Day as a group at a chowder house on the water. They dined on seafood chili chowder, crabmeat and lobster rolls, fried oysters, and salad.

Now it was time to resume life with a little less madness.

Grace plopped down in a recliner. "Happiest week of my life." She backtracked. "Other than when I married Brince and we went on our honeymoon."

"You've said this before and it needs to be said again, Brince is up in Heaven and pulling strings on your behalf."

Grace put a hand across her heart. "He would be so tickled about Cody giving us a grandchild."

"He IS tickled, Grace, and he'll help you spoil the little one. There will be moments when you know the spoiling is his handiwork coming through you."

"Thank you for everything, Elaina. I can't express just how much I appreciate what you've done for me and my family and for everyone else for that matter."

"You're welcome." Elaina had trouble dealing with the gushy sentiments, so she changed the subject. "Bailey is starting to respond to her new name. It took a while, but we're getting there. She finally left Stony's side and slept with me last night."

Tawny and Steph wandered into the living room.

"I don't know about the rest of you, but I'm pooped." Tawny slinked down on the sofa.

"How's the heartburn these days?" Steph asked.

"I haven't had a flare up for weeks." She gave the thumbs up.

"Great. Let's dive into some sauerkraut."

* * *

Steph returned to the table after her third trip to the ladies room.

"Why do you keep getting up and going to the restroom?"

She smoothed the front of the stretchy, knee-length black dress she'd bought for Nicholas Augustine the second's wedding. "Because I'm nervous."

Grace poked her in the shin with the toe of her high heels. "You have nothing to be nervous about. It's not your wedding."

"Nick's ex is across the room, giving me a glare."

"Glare back. Problem solved."

"Grace, I don't know the woman. She might stomp over and throw a glass of water in my face."

Tawny flicked her fingernails against her water glass. "You're one of four sassy chicks." She pulled the neckline of her dress down to expose the tattoo. "It's an all-for-one and one-for-all situation. If she messes with you, she'll suffer the wrath of your posse."

Nick returned. "I didn't mean to abandon you, Steph, honey. The head waiter needed to speak with me." The reception was being held at the country club where he was a member. They allowed him to supply the food and employ his staff from the restaurant to handle the meal, since his place wasn't big enough to accommodate three hundred people. "My ex's new boyfriend told him to package up the leftover food for them to take home. He has some nerve."

Philip made it known that Nick's bossy ex had been scowling at Steph.

"She's not scowling. That's her permanent look." Nick's laugh was sarcastic and loud. "Care to dance, beautiful?"

Again, Philip chimed in. "I thought you'd never ask."

Nick gave Steph his hand. "We should do a comedy tour."

"We'll be too busy doing a book tour."

"Right."

Nick led her to the dance floor, but turned and blew the rest of them a kiss.

"We're a strange bunch," Bart said.

Tawny looked at Elaina.

Poor Bart. He had no idea he would soon be excommunicated from the strange bunch. Tawny had made her decision known earlier in the day. 'It's not working. I like him as a person, but there's no chemistry. There was at first, but it burned out rather quickly. I don't want to lead him on.' Tonight he was getting axed. Elaina felt sorry for Bart, yet she understood where Tawny was coming from. Tonight you'd be hard pressed to believe they were a couple. No hand holding took place, there was no looking into each other's eyes with longing, and the conversation between them was scarce. Tawny wasn't feeling it and it was obvious neither was Bart. They were in each other's company, nothing more. Their mutual love for animals wasn't enough to prolong their relationship.

Philip and Grace made their way to the dance floor too.

"I'm a third wheel. I'm headed to the bar for a refill on my wine. Can I get you anything?"

"You're not a third wheel, you're a seventh wheel. And don't you dare leave."

Bart asked Tawny, "Are you afraid to be alone with me?"

"Umm…"

* * *

February vanished into thin air and March took its place.

Grace dangled a set of keys. "So this is happening."

"You not only own a bed and breakfast, you now have joint ownership in a lovely Victorian home."

Tawny snatched the keys. "You can't leave."

"Relax. I'll be living here for quite a while. We're not going to move in until the house has been rewired and new plumbing installed. That could take months. When I actually do move out, it'll be just across the street. You'll see my ugly mug every day."

"Everything's changing," Tawny sulked.

"I'm the one who fights change, not you. And I'm doing fine."

"Yeah, well, I see the sassy chicks going in opposite directions. Now is a good time to announce that I'm no longer working PRN, I've decided to be a full-time nurse at the hospital. They need me."

Elaina wasn't all that shocked. "I'm happy for you, Tawn'." She meant it. They each had their talents and things that were dear to their hearts. Tawny loved nursing.

"I know you are, but I won't be pulling my weight around here."

"You were meant to be a nurse first, bed and breakfast co-owner second. You'll be here when you can. When you can't, we'll manage."

"You mean *you'll* manage. Steph's time is split with helping Nick at the restaurant. Grace is now an art curator for Philip. I feel as though we're shirking our responsibilities to pursue separate interests. That's not fair to you."

"It's not a big deal. I'll occasionally have help."

Grace had been sitting quietly listening to the exchange. "I feel bad too."

Steph threw her two-cents in. "Tawny and Grace are right. We're leaving you high and dry." She sighed. "I really should rethink partnering up with Nick. He needs me, but so do you. The four of us promised to make this bed and breakfast a successful endeavor, and now we're trying to welch on that promise."

"Listen up, sassy bed and breakfast partners, and wine club members. You aren't letting me down or welching on promises. You're following the things ingrained in you. Tawny, patient care is where it's at for you. You'll be a nurse until you no longer can. Grace, even though banking isn't your life's calling, art seems to be. You're a late bloomer. You've found what makes you happy. Steph, I've known from day one that culinary excellence would take you places – to Nick's restaurant, a book tour, and who knows, maybe a cooking show on TV. The restaurant is a good fit. The bed and breakfast, and fitness, is my thing. More importantly, I can see the waterfront from here. When I feast my eyes on the Atlantic, I feel my mom's presence. Things are working out exactly the way they're supposed to."

Grace whimpered. "We don't see each other as often we should. Some days it's just in passing."

Elaina tasted a sip of sweet red wine. "Here's the thing with best friends - no matter how much time lapses between visits, we'll be able to pick up exactly where we left off."

Tawny sniffed back tears. "We're all staying in Portland." She pulled a tissue from the box on the counter and dabbed at her eyes. "We do seem to be coming and going at a rapid rate these days. Actually, we're doing more going than coming. My point is that we need to keep Wednesday night open, just for us. Sure, we'll have guests to tend to on some of those Wednesdays, but after they're tucked in, we'll crack open a bottle of wine...or four...and celebrate how far we've come and share our plans for the future. But mostly we'll enjoy each other's company."

A huge, contented smile tugged at the corners of Elaina's mouth. She raised her glass. "To Wednesdays!" After they clinked glasses, she left the table. "I almost forgot, I have something for you."

From the back of the utility closet, she pulled out the extra-large bag stuffed to the hilt with the things she purchased on that moose-wear shopping excursion.

"Moose hats? Awesome!" Grace pulled one on her head. "How do I look?"

"You want me say adorable. I'm going with ridiculous!" Tawny took a hat too and pulled it down to just above her eyes. "Now THIS is adorable."

Steph grinned and sat a hat cockeyed on her head.

Elaina did the same. "There's more." She took a stack of grey folded garments from the bag. "Moose sweat pants for everyone."

They laughed, but a tender moment passed between them. "We love you, Elaina. You're the best friend a girl could ever have."

"You're going to make me cry, Tawn'."

Grace and Steph seconded Tawny's statement. "We love you."

Stony and Bailey ran into the kitchen and dropped at her feet.

"I believe they're saying the same thing to you."

Tears rolled from the corners of Elaina's eyes and she had a happy heart. Life couldn't get any better – at least for now. "Let's take a picture and send it to Jess."

They cheesed it up for the camera.

Tawny showed the picture all around. This is going on our website.

~ The End ~

About the Author

Jan Romes grew up in northwest Ohio in the midst of eight zany siblings. Married to her high school sweetheart for more years than seems possible, she's also a mom, mother-in-law, and grandma.

Jan writes contemporary romance and women's fiction with sharp, witty characters who give as good as they get. The more she writes the more risk she's willing to take with her characters.

When she's not writing, you can find Jan with her nose buried in a book or engaged in some sort of activity to stay fit. She loves spending time with family and friends. A hopeless romantic, she enjoys sunsets, sappy movies, and sitting around a campfire.

Though she doesn't claim to have a green thumb, she takes pride in growing all kinds of flowers and plants.

She loves to hear from her readers and loves to discuss everything about writing, so don't be shy. Jan.romes@yahoo.com

You can follow Jan here:

Website:	www.authorjanromes.com
Blog:	www.jantheromancewriter.blogspot.com
Twitter:	www.twitter.com/JanRomes
Facebook:	www.facebook.com/jan.romes5
Goodreads:	www.goodreads.com/author/show/5240156.Jan_Romes
Amazon:	www.amazon.com/Jan-Romes/e/B005OMZICY

Other books by Jan Romes

Texas Boys Falling Fast series:
Book #1 – Married to Maggie
Book #2 – Keeping Kylee
Book #3 – Taming Tori
Book #4 – Not Without Nancy

One Small Fib
Lucky Ducks
Kiss Me
The Gift of Gray
Stay Close, Novac!
Stella in Stilettos
Three Wise Men
The Christmas Contract
Mr. August
Three Days with Molly
Big on Christmas
I'd Rather Be Growing Grapes
Wild Goose Chase
Tucked Away
Loving Lindy
Two More Miles

Wine and Sweat Pants series:
Book #1 - No Sweat Pants Allowed – Wine Club
Book #2 - Sipping Sangria
Book #3 - Merlot in Maine

Made in United States
Troutdale, OR
04/08/2025